"I should like to make you a proposal..."

At Arabella's look of astonishment, Titus added kindly, "Don't look so surprised. I should like you to consider marrying me."

Arabella had no doubts about it—Dr. Taverner had been overworking and had had a brainstorm— he didn't know what he was saying. She would ignore the whole thing....

Betty Neels spent her childhood and youth in Devonshire before training as a nurse and midwife. She was an army nursing sister during the war, married a Dutchman and subsequently lived in Holland for fourteen years. She lives with her husband in Dorset, and has a daughter and grandson. Her hobbies are reading, animals, old buildings and writing. Betty started to write on retirement from nursing, incited by a lady in a library bemoaning the lack of romantic novels.

Books by Betty Neels

HARLEQUIN ROMANCE
3315—A GIRL IN A MILLION
3323—AT ODDS WITH LOVE
3339—THE AWAKENED HEART
3363—A SECRET INFATUATION

Don't miss any of our special offers. Write to us at the following address for information on our newest releases.

Harlequin Reader Service
U.S.: 3010 Walden Ave., P.O. Box 1325, Buffalo, NY 14269
Canadian: P.O. Box 609, Fort Erie, Ont. L2A 5X3

DEAREST LOVE
Betty Neels

Harlequin Books

TORONTO • NEW YORK • LONDON
AMSTERDAM • PARIS • SYDNEY • HAMBURG
STOCKHOLM • ATHENS • TOKYO • MILAN
MADRID • WARSAW • BUDAPEST • AUCKLAND

ISBN 0-373-03355-9

DEAREST LOVE

Copyright © 1995 by Betty Neels.

First North American Publication 1995.

All rights reserved. Except for use in any review, the reproduction or
utilization of this work in whole or in part in any form by any electronic,
mechanical or other means, now known or hereafter invented, including
xerography, photocopying and recording, or in any information storage
or retrieval system, is forbidden without the written permission of the
publisher, Harlequin Enterprises Limited, 225 Duncan Mill Road,
Don Mills, Ontario, Canada M3B 3K9.

All characters in this book have no existence outside the imagination of
the author and have no relation whatsoever to anyone bearing the same
name or names. They are not even distantly inspired by any individual
known or unknown to the author, and all incidents are pure invention.

This edition published by arrangement with Harlequin Enterprises B.V.

® and TM are trademarks of the publisher. Trademarks indicated with
® are registered in the United States Patent and Trademark Office, the
Canadian Trade Marks Office and in other countries.

Printed in U.S.A.

CHAPTER ONE

Dear Sir,

With reference to your advertisement in this week's *Lady* magazine, I wish to apply for the post of Caretaker/Housekeeper.

I am twenty-seven years of age, single with no dependants, and have several years' experience in household management including washing, ironing, cleaning and cooking. I am a cordon bleu cook. I have a working knowledge of minor electrical and plumbing faults. I am able to take messages and answer the telephone.

I would wish to bring my cat with me.

Yours faithfully,
Arabella Lorimer

IT WAS the last letter to be read by the elderly man sitting at his desk in his consulting-room, a large apartment on the ground floor of a Regency house, one of a terrace, in Wigmore Street, London. He read it for a second time, gave a rumble of laughter, and added it to the pile before him. There were twelve applicants in all and Arabella Lorimer was the only one to enclose references—the only one to write legibly, too, neatly setting down all the relevant facts. It was a pity that she wasn't a man...

He began to read the letters again and was interrupted halfway through by the entry of his partner. Dr Titus Tavener came unhurriedly into the room, a very tall man with broad shoulders and a massive person. He was handsome with a high-bridged nose, a firm mouth and rather cold blue eyes. His hair, once fair, was pepper and salt, despite which he looked younger than his forty years.

Dr James Marshall, short and stout and almost bald, greeted him with pleasure. 'Just the man I want. The applications for the caretaker's post—I have them here; I've spent the last hour reading them. I've decided which one I shall accept. Do read them, Titus, and give me your opinion. Not that it will make any difference to my choice.' He chortled as Dr Tavener sat himself down and picked up the little pile of letters. He read them through, one after the other, and then gathered them neatly together.

'There are one or two possibles: the ex-bus driver—although he admits to asthma attacks—then this Mrs Butler.' He glanced at the letter in his hand. 'But is she quite the type to open the door? Of course the joker in the pack is Miss Arabella Lorimer and her cat. Most unsuitable.'

'Why?'

'Obviously a maiden lady down on her luck. I don't think I believe her skills are quite what she claims them to be. I'd hesitate to leave a stopped-up drainpipe or a blown fuse to her ladylike hands.'

His partner laughed. 'Titus, I can only hope that one day before it's too late you will meet a woman who will turn you sides to middle and then tramp all over you.'

Dr Tavener smiled. 'Unlikely. Perhaps I have been rather hard on the lady. There is always the possibility that she is an Amazon with a tool-kit.'

'Well, you will soon know. I've decided that she might do.'

Dr Tavener got up and strolled to the window and stood looking out on to the quiet street. 'And why not? Mrs Lane will be glad to leave. Her arthritis isn't getting any better and she's probably longing to go and live with her daughter. She'll take her furniture with her, I suppose? Do we furnish the place?'

'It depends—Miss Lorimer may have her own stuff.' Dr Marshall pushed back his chair. 'We've a busy day tomorrow; I'll see if your Amazon can come for an interview at five o'clock. Will you be back by then?'

'Unlikely—the clinic is overbooked as it is. In any case, I'm dining out.' He turned to look at his partner. 'I dare say you've made a good choice, James.' He strolled to the door. 'I've some paperwork to deal with. Shall I send Miss Baird home? You're going yourself? I shall be here for another hour yet—see you in the morning.'

He went to his own consulting-room, going through the elegant waiting-room with a smile and a nod for their shared receptionist Miss Baird, before going down the passage, past the stairs to the basement and his separate suite. This comprised a small waiting-room, a treatment-room where his nurse worked and his own room facing the garden at the back of the house. A small, narrow garden but well-tended and bright with early autumn flowers. He gave it a brief look before drawing the first of the patients' notes waiting for his attention towards him.

Dr Marshall read Miss Arabella Lorimer's letter once more and rang for Miss Baird. 'Send a note by special messenger, will you? To this address. Tell the lady to come here at five o'clock tomorrow afternoon. A pity she hasn't a telephone.' He got up and switched off his desk light. 'I'm going home, Miss Baird. Dr Tavener will be working for some time yet, but check that he's still here before you leave.' He nodded and smiled at her. 'Go as soon as you've got that message seen to.'

He went home himself then, to his wife and family, and much later Dr Tavener got into his Rolls-Royce and drove himself home to his charming house overlooking the canal in Little Venice.

Arabella read Dr Marshall's somewhat arbitrary note sitting in the kitchen. It was a small, damp room, overlooking a weary-looking patch of grass and some broken fencing, but she preferred it to the front room where her landlady sat of a Sunday afternoon. It housed the lady's prized possessions and Arabella hadn't been invited in there because of her cat Percy, who would ruin the furniture. She hadn't minded; she had been grateful that Billy Westlake, the village postman, had persuaded his aunt, Miss Pimm, to take

her in for a few days while she found a job and somewhere to live.

It hadn't been easy leaving Colpin-cum-Witham,
but it had been necessary. Her parents had died
together in a car accident and only then had she discovered that her home wasn't to be hers any longer;
it had been mortgaged to the hilt and she had to leave.
There was almost no money. She sold all but the basic
furniture that she might need and, since there was no
hope of working in or near the village and distant
aunts and uncles, while full of good advice, made no
offer to help her, she took herself and Percy to
London. She had no wish to live there but, as the
postman had said, it was a vast city and somewhere
there must be work. She had soon realised that
the only work she was capable of was domestic. She
had no skills other than cordon bleu cooking and,
since she had never needed to work in any capacity,
she had no experience—something which employers
demanded.

Now she read the brief letter again; she had applied
almost in desperation, anxious to get away from Miss
Pimm's scarcely veiled impatience to get rid of her
and Percy. She had agreed to take them in for a few
days but it was already a week and, as she had said
to Arabella, she was glad of the money but she was
one who kept herself to herself and didn't fancy
strangers in her home.

Arabella sat quietly, not allowing herself to be too
hopeful but all the same allowing herself to picture
the basement room which went with the job. She
would furnish it with her own bits and pieces and with
any luck there would be some kind of a garden behind
the house where Percy could take the air. She went

up to her little bedroom with Percy at her heels and inspected her small stock of clothes. To be suitably dressed was important.

She arrived at Wigmore Street with two minutes to spare—the clocks were striking the hour as Miss Baird ushered her into Dr Marshall's consulting-room. He was sitting behind his desk as she went in and put down his pen to peer at her over his glasses. Just for a moment he was silent, then he said, 'Miss Lorimer? Please sit down. I must confess I was expecting someone more—more robust...'

Arabella seated herself without fuss—a small, nicely plump girl with mousy hair pinned on top of her head, an ordinary face and a pair of large grey eyes, thickly fringed. Anyone less like a caretaker it would be hard to find, reflected Dr Marshall with an inward chuckle, and just wait until Titus saw her.

He said pleasantly, 'I read your letter with interest, Miss Lorimer. Will you tell me about your last job?'

'I haven't had one. I've always lived at home—my mother was delicate and my father was away a good deal; he had his own business. I always did the house-keeping and dealt with minor repairs around the house.'

He nodded. 'Why do you want this job?'

She was sitting very quietly—no fidgeting, he noticed thankfully.

'My parents were killed recently in a car accident and now my home is no longer mine. We lived at Colpin-cum-Witham in southern Wiltshire; there is no work there for someone with no qualifications.' She paused. 'I need somewhere to live and domestic work seems to be the answer. I have applied for several jobs but they won't allow me to have Percy.'

'Percy?'

'My cat.'

'Well, I see no objection to a cat as long as he stays in your room—he can have the use of the garden, of course. But do you suppose that you are up to the work? You are expected to clean these rooms—mine, the reception and waiting-room, the passage and the stairs, my partner's rooms—and polish all the furniture and brass, and the front door, then answer the bell during our working hours, empty the bins, lock up and unlock in the mornings... Are you of a nervous disposition?'

'No, I don't think so.'

'Good. Oh, and if there is no one about you will answer the telephone, run errands and take messages.' He gave her a shrewd glance. 'A bit too much for you, eh?'

'Certainly not, Dr Marshall. I dare say I should call you sir? I would be glad to come and work for you.'

'Shall we give it a month's trial? Mrs Lane who is retiring should be in her room now. If you will go with Miss Baird she will introduce you. Come back here, if you please, so that we can make final arrangements.'

The basement wasn't quite what Arabella had imagined but it had possibilities. It was a large room; its front windows gave a view of passing feet and were heavily barred but the windows at the other end of the room, although small, could be opened. There was a door loaded down with bolts and locks and chains beside them, leading out to a small paved area with the garden beyond. At one side there was a door

opening into a narrow passage with a staircase leading
to the floor above and ending in another heavy door
and, beside the staircase, a very small kitchen and an
even smaller shower-room. Mrs Lane trotted ahead
of her, pointing out the amenities. 'Of course I shall
'ave ter take me things with me, ducks—going up ter
me daughter, yer see; she's got a room for me.'

'I have some furniture, Mrs Lane,' said Arabella
politely. 'I only hope to be able to make it as cosy as
you have done.'

Mrs Lane preened. 'Well, I've me pride, love. A
bit small and young, aint yer?'

'Well, I'm very strong and used to housework.
When did you want to leave, Mrs Lane?'

'Just as soon as yer can get 'ere. Bin 'appy 'ere, I
'ave, but I'm getting on a bit—the stairs is a bit much.
'Is nibs 'as always 'ad a girl come in ter answer the
door, which save me feet.' She chuckled. ''E won't
need 'er now!'

Back with Dr Marshall, Arabella, bidden to sit, sat.

'Well, want to come here and work?'

'Yes, I do and I will do my best to satisfy you, sir.'

'Good. Fix up dates and so on with Mrs Lane and
let me know when you're going to come.' He added
sharply, 'There must be no gap between Mrs Lane
going and you coming, understand.'

Outside in the street she went looking for a telephone box to ring the warehouse in Sherborne and
arrange for her furniture to be brought to London.
It was a matter of urgency and for once good fortune
was on her side. There was a load leaving for London
in three days' time and her few things could be sent
with it and at a much smaller cost than she had expected. She went back to Mrs Lane, going down the

few steps to the narrow door by the barred window and explaining carefully, 'If I might come here some time during the morning and you leave in the afternoon, could we manage to change over without upsetting your routine here?'

'Don't see why not, ducks. Me son-in-law's coming with a van so I'll clear off as soon as yer 'ere.'

'Then I'll let Dr Marshall know.'

'Do that. I'll 'ave ter see 'im for me wages—I'll tell 'im likewise.'

Back at Miss Pimm's, Arabella told her that she would be leaving in three days and ate her supper—fish and chips from the shop on the corner—and went to bed, explaining to Percy as she undressed that he would soon have a home of his own again. He was a docile cat but he hadn't been happy at Miss Pimm's; it was a far cry from the roomy house and garden that he had always lived in. Now he curled up on the end of her narrow bed and went to sleep, instinct telling him that better times were in store.

Dr Marshall sat at his desk for some time doing nothing after Arabella had gone. Presently he gave a rich chuckle and when Miss Baird came in he asked her, 'Well, what do you think of our new caretaker?'

Miss Baird gave him a thoughtful look. 'A very nice young lady, sir. I only hope she's up to all that hard housework.'

'She assures me that she is a most capable worker. She will start in three days' time and I must be sure and be here when Dr Tavener sees her for the first time.'

It wasn't until the next morning, discussing a difficult case with his partner, that Dr Marshall had the chance to mention that he had engaged a new care-taker. 'She will start in two days' time—with her cat.'

Dr Tavener laughed. 'So she turned out to be suitable for the job? Let us hope that she is quicker at answering the doorbell and emptying the waste-paper baskets.'

'Oh, I imagine she will be.' Dr Marshall added slyly, 'After all, she is young.'

'As long as she does her work properly.' Dr Tavener was already engrossed in the notes in his hand and spoke without interest.

Despite misgivings that her furniture wouldn't arrive, that Percy would disappear at the last minute or that Dr Marshall would have second thoughts about em-ploying her, Arabella moved herself, her cat and her few possessions into the basement of Wigmore Street without mishap. True, empty it looked pretty grim and rather dirty, but once the floor had been cleaned and the windows washed, the cobwebs removed from the darker corners, she could see possibilities. With the help of the removal men she put her bed in a corner of the room, put a small table and chair under the back window and stacked everything else tidily against a wall. Her duties were to commence in the morning and she conned Mrs Lane's laboriously written list of duties before she made up the bed, settled Percy in his cardboard box and rolled up her sleeves.

There was plenty of hot water and Mrs Lane had left a variety of mops and brushes in the cupboard by the stairs. Arabella set to with a will; this was to be her home—hers and Percy's—and she intended to make it as comfortable as possible. Cleanliness came before comfort. She scrubbed and swept and polished and by evening was satisfied with her work.

She cooked her supper on the newly cleaned stove—beans on toast and an egg—gave Percy his meal and sat at the table, well pleased with her efforts, while she drank her tea and then made a list of the things she still needed. It was not a long list but she would have to buy a little at a time each pay-day. Her rather muddled calculations showed her that it would be Christmas before she had all she wanted but that didn't worry her—after the last awful months this was all that she could wish for.

She washed her dishes and opened the back door with Percy tucked under one arm. The garden was surrounded by a high brick wall and ringed by flower-beds but there was a good-sized strip of lawn as well. She set Percy down and watched him explore, at first with caution and then with pleasure. After Miss Pimm's little yard this was bliss...

She perched on a small rustic seat, tired now but happy. It had been a fine day but it was getting chilly now and dusk had dimmed the colourful garden. She scooped up Percy and went back indoors and then, mindful of Mrs Lane's instructions, went up the stairs and inspected each room in turn, making sure that the windows were closed and locked, the doors bolted and all the lights turned out. The two floors above her were lived in, Mrs Lane had told her, by a neurologist and his wife. They had a side entrance, a small door at the front of the house, and although he was retired he still saw the occasional patient. 'But nothing ter do with us,' Mrs Lane had said. 'Yer won't ever see them.'

All the same it was nice to think that the house wasn't quite empty. She took her time in locking up, looking at everything so that she would know where things were in the morning and, being of a practical turn of mind, she searched until she found the stopcock, the fire-extinguisher and the gas and electricity meters. She also searched for and eventually found a box containing such useful things as a hammer, nails, spare light-bulbs, a wrench and adhesive tape. They were hidden away in a small dark cupboard and she felt sure that no one had been near it for a very long time. She put everything back carefully and reminded herself to ask for a plunger. Blocked sinks could be a nuisance, especially where people would be constantly washing their hands. Satisfied at last, she went back to her room, had a shower and got into bed, and Percy, uninvited but very welcome, climbed on too and settled on her feet.

She was up early, tidied the room and made the bed, fed Percy and escorted him into the garden, ate a sketchy breakfast and took herself off upstairs, wearing her new nylon overall.

There was everything she might need—a vacuum cleaner, polish and dusters. She emptied the wastepaper baskets, set the chairs to rights, arranged the magazines just so, polished the front door-knocker and opened the windows. It looked very nice when she had finished but a little austere. She went back downstairs and out into the garden; she cut Michaelmas daisies, dahlias and one or two late roses. She bore them back, found three vases, arranged the flowers in them and put one in each of the consulting-rooms and the last one in the waiting-room. They made all the difference, she considered, and realised that she had overlooked the second waiting-room. Back in the garden, she cut asters this time, arranged them in a deep bowl and put them on the table flanked by the magazines.

She hadn't met Dr Marshall's partner; she hoped he was as nice as that gentleman.

She went back to the basement then, tidied herself, made sure that her hair was neat and when the doorbell rang went to answer it. It was Dr Marshall's nurse, who had introduced herself as Joyce Pierce and then exclaimed, 'You're the new caretaker? Well, I must say you're a bit of a surprise. Do you think you'll like it?'

'Well, yes. I can live here, you see, and I don't mind housework.'

She was shutting the door when the second nurse arrived, small and dark and pretty. 'The caretaker?' she asked and raised her eyebrows. 'Whatever's come over Dr Marshall?' She nodded at Arabella. 'I'm Madge Simmons. I work for Dr Tavener.' She spoke rather frostily. 'Come on, Joyce, we've time for a cup of tea.'

The first patient wouldn't arrive until nine o'clock so Arabella sped downstairs. There was still a tea-chest of bed-linen, table-linen and curtains to unpack. As soon as she could she would get some net and hang it in the front window, shutting off all those feet...

At a quarter to nine she went upstairs again. There was no sign of the two nurses, although she could hear voices, and she stood uncertainly in the hall—to turn and face the door as it was opened. The man who entered seemed to her to be enormous. The partner, she thought, eyeing his elegance and his good looks and was very startled when he observed, 'Good lord, the caretaker!' and laughed.

The laugh annoyed her. She wished him good morning in a small frosty voice and went down to her room, closing the door very quietly behind her. 'He's what one would call a magnificent figure of a man,' she told Percy, 'and also a very rude one!'

The front doorbell rang then, and she went upstairs to admit the first patient. For the next hour or so she trotted up and down the stairs a dozen times until finally she shut the door on the last patient and Miss Baird came to tell her that Dr Marshall wanted to see her.

He eyed her over his specs. 'Morning, Miss Lorimer. Where did you get the flowers?'

The question surprised her. 'From the garden—only the ones at the back of the beds...'

'Nice idea. Finding your feet?'

'Yes, thank you, sir.'

'Miss Baird will tell you what to do when we've gone. We'll be back this afternoon, one or other of us, but not until three o'clock. You're free once you've tidied up and had your lunch, but be back here by quarter to. We sometimes work in the evening, but not often. Did Mrs Lane tell you where the nearest shops were?'

'No, but I can find them.'

He nodded and looked up as the door opened and Dr Tavener came in. 'Ah, here is my partner, Dr Tavener. This is our new caretaker.'

'We have already met,' said Arabella in a chilly voice. 'If that is all, sir?'

'Not quite all,' said Dr Tavener. 'I owe you an apology, Miss...'

'Lorimer, sir.'

'Miss Lorimer. I was most discourteous but I can assure you that my laughter was not at you as a person.'

'It was of no consequence, sir.' She gave him a fierce look from her lovely eyes which belied the sober reply and looked at Dr Marshall.

'Yes. Yes, go along, Miss Lorimer. If you need anything, don't hesitate to ask.'

A practical girl, Arabella paused at the door. 'I should like a plunger, sir.' She saw that he was puzzled. 'It is used for unstopping sinks and drains. They're not expensive.'

Not a muscle of Dr Tavener's handsome features moved; he asked gravely, 'Have we a blocked sink, Miss Lorimer?'

'No, but it's something which usually happens at an awkward time—it would be nice to have one handy.'

Dr Marshall spoke. 'Yes, yes, of course. Very wise. We have always called in a plumber, I believe.'

'It isn't always necessary,' she told him kindly.

'Ask Miss Baird to deal with it as you go, will you?'

Dr Tavener closed the door behind her and sat down. 'A paragon,' he observed mildly. 'With a plunger too! Do we know anything about her, James?'

'She comes from a place called Colpin-cum-Witham in Wiltshire. Parents killed in a car crash and—for some reason not specified—she had to leave her home. Presumably no money. Excellent references from the local parson and doctor. She's on a month's trial.' He smiled. 'Have you got flowers in your room too?'

'Yes, indeed.' He added, 'Don't let us forget that new brooms sweep clean.'

'You don't like her?'

'My dear James, I don't know her and it is most unlikely that I shall see enough of her to form an opinion.' He got up and went to look out of the window. 'I thought I'd drive up to Leeds—the consultation isn't until the afternoon. I'll go on to Birmingham from there and come back on the following day. Miss Baird has fixed my appointments so that I have a couple of days free.'

Dr Marshall nodded. 'That's fine. I'm not too keen on going to that seminar in Oslo. Will you go?'

'Certainly. It's two weeks ahead, isn't it? If I fly over it will only take three days.' He glanced at his watch. 'I'd better do some work; I've that article to finish for the *Lancet*.' He went to the door. 'I've two patients for this evening, by the way.'

As for Arabella, she went back to her room, had lunch, fed Percy and, after a cautious look round, went into the garden with him, unaware that Dr Tavener was at his desk at the window. He watched her idly, admired Percy's handsome grey fur, and then forgot her.

Miss Baird had been very helpful. There were, she had told Arabella, one or two small shops not five minutes' walk away down a small side-street. Arabella put on her jacket and, armed with a shopping-basket, set off to discover them. They were tucked away from the quiet prosperous streets with their large houses— a newsagents, a greengrocer and a small general store. Sufficient for her needs. She stocked up with enough food for a couple of days, bought herself a newspaper and then went back to Wigmore Street. On Saturday, she promised herself, she would spend her free afternoon shopping for some of the things on her list. She was to be paid each week, Miss Baird had told her and, although she should save for an uncertain future, there were some small comforts she would need. She would have all Sunday to work without interruption.

After that first day the week went quickly; by the end of it Arabella had found her feet. She saw little of the nurses and still less of Dr Marshall, and nothing at all of his partner. It was only when she went to Miss Baird to collect her wages that she overheard one of the nurses remark that Dr Tavener would be back on Monday. 'And a good thing too,' she had added, 'for his appointments book is full. He's away again in a couple of weeks for that seminar in Oslo.'

'He doesn't get much time for his love-life, does he?' laughed the other nurse.

Arabella, with her pay-packet a delightful weight in her pocket, even felt vague relief that he would be going away again. She had been careful to keep out of his way, although she wasn't sure why, and the last two days while he had been away she had felt much more comfortable. 'It's because he's so large,' she told Percy, and fell to counting the contents of her pay-packet.

While her parents had been alive she had lived a comfortable enough life. There had always seemed to be money; she had never been spoilt but she had never gone without anything she had needed or asked for. Now she held in her hand what was, for her, quite a large sum of money and she must plan to spend it carefully. New clothes were for the moment out of the question. True, those she had were of good quality and although her wardrobe was small it was more than adequate for her needs. She got paper and pen and checked her list . . .

It took her until one o'clock to clear up after the Saturday morning appointments and then there was the closing and the locking up to do, the answering machine to set, the few cups and saucers to wash and dry, the gas and electricity to check. She ate a hasty lunch, saw to Percy's needs then changed into her brown jersey skirt and the checked blouson jacket which went with it, stuck her rather tired feet into the Italian loafers she had bought with her mother in the happy times she tried not to remember too often, and, with her shoulder-bag swinging, caught a bus to Tottenham Court Road.

The tea-chests had yielded several treasures: curtains which could be cut to fit the basement windows and make cushion covers, odds and ends of china and kitchenware, a clock—she remembered it from the kitchen; a small radio—still working; some books and, right at the bottom, a small thin mat which would look nice before the gas fire.

She needed to buy needles and sewing cottons, net curtains, scissors and more towels, shampoo and some soap and, having purchased these, she poked around the cheaper shops until she found what she wanted: a roll of thin matting for the floor—it would be awkward to carry but it would be worth the effort. So, for that matter, would the tin of paint in a pleasing shade of pale apricot. She added a brush and, laden down with her awkward shopping, took a bus back to Wigmore Street.

Back in the basement again, she changed into an elderly skirt and jumper and went into the garden with Percy. It was dusk already and there were no lights on in the rooms above. The house seemed very silent and empty and there was a chilly wind. Percy disliked wind; he hurried back indoors and she locked and bolted the door before getting her supper and feeding him. Her meal over, she washed up and went upstairs to check carefully that everything was just as it should be before going back to lay the matting.

It certainly made a difference to the dim little room; the matting almost covered the mud-coloured flooring, and when she had spread an old-fashioned chenille tablecloth over the round table its cheerful crimson brightened the place further. It had been at the bottom of one of the tea-chests, wrapped around some of the china, and the curtains were of the same crimson. It was too late to start them that evening but she could at least sew the net curtains she had bought. It was bedtime by the time she had done that, run a wire through their tops, banged in some small nails and hung them across the bars of the windows. She went to bed then, pleased with her efforts.

She woke in the middle of the night, for the moment forgetful of where she was and then, suddenly overcome with grief and loneliness, cried herself to sleep again. She woke in the morning to find Percy sitting on her chest, peering down at her face—part of her old life—and she at once sat up in bed, dismissing self-pity. The walls had to be painted and if there was time she would begin on the curtains...

'We have a home,' she told Percy as she dressed, 'and money in our pockets and work to keep us busy. It's a lovely morning; we'll go into the garden.'

There was a faint chill in the air and there was a Sunday morning quiet. She thought of all the things she would do, the places she would visit in the coming weeks, and feeling quite cheerful got their breakfasts.

She had covered the drab, discoloured wallpaper by the late afternoon and the room looked quite different. The pale apricot gave the place light and warmth and she ate her combined tea and supper in great content.

The smell was rather overpowering; she opened the door to the garden despite the chilly evening and cut up the curtains ready to sew, fired with enthusiasm. As she wielded the scissors she planned what to buy with her next pay-packet: a bedspread, a table-lamp, a picture or two—the list was neverending!

CHAPTER TWO

DR TAVERNER, arriving the next morning, saw the net curtains and grinned. Unlike Mrs Lane, the new care-taker disliked the view from her window. Mrs Lane, on the other hand, had once told him that she found the sight of passing feet very soothing.

There were fresh flowers on his desk and there wasn't a speck of dust to be seen; the wastepaper basket was empty and the elegant gas fire had been lighted. He sat down to study the notes of his first patient and hoped that such a satisfactory state of affairs would continue. She was quite unsuitable, of course; either she would find the work too much for her or she would find something more suitable.

Arabella, fortunately unaware of these conjectures, went about her duties with brisk efficiency. Miss Baird had wished her a cheerful good morning when she had arrived, even the two nurses had smiled as she opened the door to them, and after that for some time she was opening and closing the door for patients, ignored for the most part—a small, rather colourless creature, not worth a second glance.

She had no need to go to the shops at lunchtime—the milkman had left milk and she had everything she needed for making bread. She made the dough, kneaded it and set it to rise before the gas fire while she started on the curtains. She was as handy with her needle as she was with her cooking and she had

25

them ready by the time she had to go back upstairs to let in the first of the afternoon patients. She would hang them as soon as everyone had gone later on.

By half-past five the place was quiet. The last patient had been seen on his way, the nurses followed soon afterwards and lastly Miss Baird. Dr Marshall had already gone and she supposed that Dr Tavener had gone too. It would take her an hour to tidy up and make everything secure for the night but she would hang the curtains first...

They looked nice. Cut from the crimson curtains which had hung in the dining-room of her old home they were of heavy dull brocade, lined too, so that she had had very little sewing to do. She admired them drawn across the hated bars, and went upstairs to begin the business of clearing up.

She had a plastic bag with her and emptied the wastepaper baskets first—a job Miss Baird had impressed upon her as never to be forgotten. She went around putting things in their proper places, shaking the cushions in the waiting-room chairs, turning off lights, picking up magazines and putting them back on the table. She went along to Dr Tavener's rooms presently and was surprised to find the light on in his consulting-room.

He was at his desk and didn't look up. 'Be good enough to come back later, Miss Lorimer. I shall be here for another hour.'

She went away without saying anything and went back to the basement and began to get her supper. Percy, comfortably full, sat before the fire and the bread was in the oven. She whipped up a cheese soufflé, set the table with a cloth and put a small vase of flowers she had taken from the garden in its centre.

She had been allowed to take essential things when she left her home—knives and spoons and forks and a plate or two. She had taken the silver and her mother's Coalport china plates and cups and saucers; she had taken the silver pepperpot and salt cellar too, and a valuable teapot—Worcester. She would have liked to have taken the silver one but she hadn't quite dared—though she had taken the Waterford crystal jug and two wine-glasses.

She ate her soufflé presently, bit into an apple and made coffee before taking the bread from the oven. By then almost two hours had elapsed. She put her overall on once again and went upstairs to meet Dr Tavener as he left his rooms.

He stopped short when he saw her. 'Something smells delicious . . .'

'I have been making bread,' said Arabella, cool and polite and wishing that he would hurry up and go so that she could get her work done.

'Have you, indeed? And do I detect the smell of paint? Oh, do not look alarmed. It is very faint; I doubt if anyone noticed it.' He stared down at her. 'You are not afraid to be here alone?'

'No, sir.'

He wished her goodnight then, and she closed the door after him, bolting it and locking it securely. He paused on the pavement and looked down at the basement window. She had drawn the curtains and there was only a faint line of light showing. He frowned; he had no interest in the girl but living in that poky basement didn't seem right . . . He shrugged his shoulders; after all, she had chosen the job.

A week went by and Arabella had settled into a routine which ensured that she was seldom seen during working hours. Tidying Miss Baird's desk one evening, she had seen the list of patients for the following day, which gave her a good idea as to the times of their arrival. Now she checked each evening's list, for not all the patients came early in the day—once or twice there was no one until after ten o'clock, which gave her time to sweep and dust her own room and have a cup of coffee in peace. Nicely organised, she found life bearable if not exciting and, now that her room was very nearly as she wished it, she planned to spend part of her Sundays in the London parks. She missed the country. Indeed, come what may, she had promised herself that one day she would leave London but first she had to save some money before finding a job near her old home.

'We will go back,' she assured Percy, 'I promise you. Only we must stay here for a while—a year, perhaps two—just until we have enough money to feel safe.'

Only Dr Marshall came in on the Monday morning. Dr Tavener would be in directly after lunch, Miss Baird told her. He was taking a clinic at one of the nearby hospitals that morning. 'He's got a lot of patients too,' she warned Arabella. 'He probably won't be finished until early evening—he doesn't mind if he works late; he's not married and hasn't any ties.' She added kindly, 'If you want to run round to the shops I'll see to the phone and the door.'

'Thank you. If I could just get some vegetables? I can be back in fifteen minutes.'

'Don't hurry. You do cook proper meals for yourself?'

'Oh, yes. I have plenty of time in the evening.'

It was a cheerless morning, not quite October and already chilly. Arabella nipped smartly to the row of little shops, chose onions and turnips and carrots with care, bought meat from the butcher next door and hurried back. A casserole would be easy, she could leave it to cook gently and it wouldn't spoil however late she might have her supper. A few dumplings, she reflected and a bouquet garni. It would do for the following day too.

She prepared it during the lunch hour, gave Percy his share of the meat and tidied herself ready to open the door for the first of Dr Tavener's patients.

The last patient went just before six o'clock and Arabella, having already tidied Dr Marshall's rooms, started to close the windows and lock up. There was still no sign of Dr Tavener when she had done this so she went down to the basement, set the table for her supper and checked the casserole in the oven. It was almost ready; she turned off the gas and set the dish on top of the stove, lifted the lid and gently stirred the contents—they smelled delicious.

Dr Tavener, on the point of leaving, paused in the hall, his splendid nose flaring as he sniffed the air. He opened the door to the basement and sniffed again and then went down the stairs and knocked at the door.

There was silence for a moment before he was bidden to enter—to discover Arabella standing facing the door, looking uncertain.

Neither of them spoke for a moment. Arabella was surprised to see him—she hadn't known who it was and had secretly been a little frightened—and as for Dr Tavener, he stood looking around him before remarking, 'Dear me, you have been busy and to very good effect.' He glanced at the table, nicely laid with a white cloth, the silver, one of the Coalport plates, a Waterford glass and a small vase of flowers. Their new caretaker was, indeed, a little out of the common. 'I hope I didn't startle you; something smelled so delicious that I had to see what it was. Your supper?'

She nodded.

He said with amusement, 'Are you a cordon bleu cook as well as a plumber?'

'Yes.'

'Surely if that is the case you could have found a more congenial post?'

'No one would have Percy.'

Dr Tavener studied the cat sitting before the little fire staring at him. 'A handsome beast.' And then, since their conversation was making no progress at all, 'Goodnight, Miss Lorimer.' As he turned away he added, 'You will lock up?'

'I have been waiting to do so, sir.' Her voice was tart.

His smile dismissed that. 'As long as you carry out your duties, Miss Lorimer.'

He had gone then, as quietly as he had come.

'He isn't just rude,' Arabella told Percy. 'He's very rude!'

When she heard the front door close she put the casserole in the oven again and went upstairs to clear up his rooms, close the windows and turn the key in the door before the lengthy business of locking and bolting the front door. Only then did she go back to her delayed supper.

Sitting by the gas fire later, sewing at the cushion covers, she allowed her thoughts to dwell upon Dr Tavener. He didn't like her, that was obvious, and yet

he had come down to her room—something Dr
Marshall would never think of doing. Perhaps she
should have been more friendly, but were caretakers
supposed to be friendly with their employers? She
doubted that. He unsettled her. While her parents had
been alive she had had friends, cheerful young men
and women of her own age, but none of the young
men had fallen in love with her, nor had she been
particularly attracted to any of them. Dr Tavener
wasn't like any of them. It wasn't only his good
looks—perhaps it was because he was older. She gave
up thinking about him and turned her attention to her
work.

She had only brief glimpses of him for the rest of
that week and beyond a terse greeting he didn't speak
to her. On the other hand, Dr Marshall, while
evincing no interest at all in her private life, was always
friendly if they chanced to encounter each other.

Then Dr Tavener went to Oslo, his nurse took a
holiday and Arabella found herself with less to do.
True, she checked his rooms night and morning, but
there was no need to Hoover and polish now he was
away. There were fewer doorbells to answer too, so
she had time to spare in which to make apple chutney
from the windfalls dropping from the small old tree
at the bottom of the garden. She had, of course, asked
Dr Marshall first if she might have them and he had
said yes, adding that he had had no idea that they
could be used. So for several evenings there was a
pleasant smell of cooking apples coming from the
basement. She made bread too, and a batch of scones;
and buns with currents—nicely iced; and a sponge
cake, feather-light. The tiny old-fashioned pantry, its

shelves empty for so long for Mrs Lane had only fancied food out of tins, began to fill nicely.

Dr Tavener was due back on the following day, Miss Baird told her. Not until the late afternoon, though, so there would be no patients for him. 'And I daresay he'll go straight home and come in the next morning.'

So Arabella gave his rooms a final dusting. There were still some Doris pinks in the garden; she arranged some in a glass vase and added some sprigs of lavender and some veronica. The room was cool so they would stay fresh overnight—she must remember to turn the central heating on in the morning and light the gas fire. She put everything ready for the nurse too, so that she could make herself a cup of tea when she arrived, then she went round checking the windows and the doors, and went downstairs again.

Dr Marshall had a great number of patients the next morning; she was kept busy answering the door and Dr Tavener's nurse, short-tempered for some reason, found fault with her because the central heating hadn't been turned on sooner. In the afternoon it began to rain—a steady downpour—so the patients left wet footprints over the parquet flooring and dropped their dripping umbrellas unheeding on to the two chairs which flanked the side-table. Arabella had taken a lot of trouble to clean them and polish them and now they were covered in damp spots. She would have liked to bang the door behind them as they left . . .

The house was quiet at last and she fetched her plastic bag, her dusters and polish, and lugged the Hoover from its place under the stairs. There had been no sign of Dr Tavener; he would have gone straight home as Miss Baird had suggested. Arabella bustled around, intent on getting back to her own room. Tea had been out of the question and she thought with pleasure of the supper she intended to cook—a Spanish omelette with a small salad. She had made soup yesterday, with bones and root vegetables, and she would have an apple or two and a handful of raisins. Bread and butter and a large pot of tea instead of coffee—what more could anyone want?

The weather had turned nasty, with a cold wind and heavy rain. It was a lonely sound beating on the windows; she wondered why it sounded so different from the rain on the windows of her home at Colpin-cum-Witham. There the wind used to sough through the trees—a sound she had loved. She had finished her tidying up when she remembered that the nurse had complained about the light in the waiting-room. The bulb wasn't strong enough, she had been told, and another one must replace it. She fetched it and then went to haul the step-ladder up from the basement so that she might reach the elaborate shade hanging from the ceiling.

She was on the top step when she heard the front door being opened, and a moment later Dr Tavener came into the room. He was bareheaded and carried his case in his hand. He put it down, lifted her down from the steps, took the bulb from her hand and changed it with the one already in the socket. Only then did he get down and bid her good evening.

Arabella, taken by surprise, hadn't uttered a sound. Now she found her voice and uttered a stiff thank you.

He stood looking at her. 'It's a filthy night,' he observed. 'You wouldn't be kind and make me a cup of tea or coffee—whichever is easiest?'

She started for the little kitchenette leading from his rooms but he put out a hand. 'No, no. No need here—may I not come downstairs with you?'

She eyed him uncertainly. 'Well, if you want to,' she said matter-of-factly. 'I was going to make tea.'

She went down to the basement, very conscious of him just behind her. The room looked surprisingly cosy; she had left one of the little table-lamps lit and the gas fire was on. She went to turn it up and said rather shyly, 'Please sit down, the tea won't take long.'

He sat down in the small shabby armchair and Percy got on to his knees. 'Have you had your supper? Do I smell soup?'

'Are you hungry?' She warmed the teapot and spooned in the tea.

'Ravenous. My housekeeper doesn't expect me back until the morning.' He watched her as she made the tea. 'I could go out for a meal, I suppose. Would you come with me?'

She looked up in surprise. 'Well, thank you for asking me but I've supper all ready.' She paused to think. 'You can share it if you would like to, though I'm not sure if it's quite the thing. I mean, I'm the caretaker!'

He smiled and said easily, 'You are also a splendid cook, are you not?' He got up out of his chair. 'And I don't believe there is a law against caretakers asking a guest for a meal.'

'Well, of course, put like that it seems quite...' She paused, at a loss for a word.

'Quite,' said Dr Tavener. 'What comes after the soup?'

She laid another place at the table. 'Well, a Spanish omelette with a salad. I haven't a pudding, but there is bread and butter and cheese ...'

'Home-made bread?' And when she nodded he said, 'I can think of nothing nicer. While you are cooking the omelette I shall go and get a bottle of wine. Five minutes?'

He had gone. She heard the door close behind him and the car start up. She broke three eggs into a bowl and then a fourth—he was a very large man.

The omelette was ready to cook when he got back, put a bottle on the table and asked if she had a cork-screw. It was a good wine—a red burgundy of a good vintage, its cost almost as much as half of Arabella's pay-packet. He opened it to let it breathe.

Arabella was ladling soup into the large old-fashioned soup plates which had belonged to her grandmother. Dr Tavener, sampling it, acknowledged that it was worthy of the Coalport china in which it was served.

He fetched the wine and poured it as she dished up the omelette and, warmed by its delicious fruitiness, Arabella forgot to be a caretaker and was once again a well brought-up young lady with a pleasant social life. Dr Tavener, leading her on with quiet cunning, discovered a good deal more about her than she realised. Not that he asked questions but merely put in a word here and there, egging her on gently.

They finished the omelette and sat talking over coffee and slices of bread and butter and a piece of cheese. If he found the meal a trifle out of the or-dinary way of things he gave no sign. Bread and butter, he discovered, when the bread had been baked by his hostess, was exactly the right way to finish his supper.

Being a giant of a man, he ate most of the loaf and a good deal of the butter. She would have to go to the shops the next day...

It was almost ten o'clock when he went, taking her with him so that she could lock up after him. He stood on the pavement, thinking of her polite goodnight and listening to the bolts being shot home and the key turned in the lock. He had never worried about Mrs Lane being alone in the house for the simple reason that she frequently had had various members of her family spending a few days with her, but Arabella had no one. The idea of Arabella being alone at night nagged at him all the way to his home.

It was on the following Saturday afternoon that Arabella added another member to her household. She was returning from the shops, laden with a week's supply of basic food, taking shortcuts through the narrow streets which would bring her into Wigmore Street. It had been a dull, chilly day and bid fair to lapse into early dusk bringing a fine drizzle of rain. Head bowed against the damp wind, weighed down with her shopping, she turned down a short alleyway which would take her close to Dr Marshall's rooms.

She was almost at its end when a faint movement in the gutter caused her to stop. A puppy lay there, rolled up and moving to and fro, its yelps so faint that she could hardly hear them. She put down her plastic bags and bent to take a closer look. It was a pitiful sight, thin and very wet, and someone had tied its back legs together. Arabella let out a snort of rage and knelt down the better to deal with it. The cord was tight but roughly tied; it took only a moment to untie it and scoop up the small creature, pop him on top of her shopping and carry him back to her basement.

He was a very young puppy and, even if well fed and cared for, would have had no good looks. As it was he was a sorry sight, with tiny ribs showing through his dirty coat and sores on his flanks. Notwithstanding, he lay passive on the table while she gently examined him, and even waved a very long and rat-like tail. She dumped her shopping, fetched warm water and some old cloths, and cleaned him gently, wrapped him in an old curtain and set him before the gas fire where he lay too tired to move when Percy went to examine him in his turn.

'Bread and warm milk,' said Arabella who, living alone with only a cat for company, frequently uttered her thoughts out loud, and suited the action to the words. It was received thankfully and scoffed with pathetic speed so she gave him more warm milk with some vague idea about dehydration and then, aware of Percy's indignant stare, offered him his supper too, before taking off her jacket and putting away her shopping. She got her own tea presently, pausing frequently to look at the puppy. He was sleeping, uttering small yelps as he slept, and presently Percy stretched out beside him, with the air of someone doing a good deed, and curved himself round the small skinny creature.

'That's right, Percy,' encouraged Arabella. 'He could do with a good cuddle. He'll be a handsome dog if we look after him.'

He woke presently and she gave him some of Percy's food and took him into the dark garden, and when she went off to bed she lifted him on to its foot beside Percy. He looked better already. She woke in the night and found him still sleeping, but Percy had crept up the bed and was lying beside her.

It was then that she began to wonder what Dr Marshall was going to say when he discovered that she had a dog as well as a cat. Why should she tell him? The puppy was very young—his bark would be small and until he was much stronger he might not bark at all. Indeed, he would be no trouble for some time; he was far too weak to behave as a normal puppy would. Things settled to her satisfaction, she went back to sleep until Percy's nudges woke her once more.

Being Sunday, she had the place to herself and nothing could have been more convenient. The puppy, shivering with terror, was borne out into the garden again and then given his breakfast while Percy ate his, afterwards curling up before the fire and allowing the puppy to crouch beside him. Presently Percy stretched his length before the warmth and the puppy crept even closer and went to sleep.

He slept and ate all day and by the evening he cringed only occasionally, waving his ridiculous tail in an effort to show his gratitude.

'I shall keep you,' said Arabella. 'Percy likes you and so do I! And you're more than welcome.'

The puppy, unused to a kind voice, gave a very small squeaky bark, ate a second supper and went to sleep— this time with his ugly little head on Percy's portly stomach.

Monday came and with it a nasty nervous feeling on Arabella's part, but she went about her duties as usual and by the end of the day was lulled into a sense of security by the exemplary behaviour of the puppy who, doubtless because he was still very much under the weather, did nothing other than eat the food she offered him and sleep, keeping as close to a tolerant Percy as possible.

By the end of the week he had filled out considerably although he was still quite content to curl up and sleep. He went willingly enough into the garden before anyone was about and, although the dark evenings scared him, provided Percy was nearby he ventured on to the grass and even scampered around for a few minutes.

It was carelessness due to her overconfidence that was Arabella's undoing. On the Friday evening everyone left as usual and, after a quick reconnoitre upstairs to make sure that that really was the case, she went into the garden before she tidied the rooms. It was a fine clear evening and not quite dark and she took her torch and walked down the path while the animals pottered on the grass.

Dr Tavener, returning to fetch a forgotten paper, trod quietly through the empty rooms and, since there was still some light left, didn't bother to turn on his desk lamp. He knew where the paper was and he had picked it up and turned to go again when he glanced out of his window.

Arabella stood below, her torch shining on the animals.

'Well, I'm damned,' said Dr Tavener softly and watched her shepherd them indoors before going silently and very quickly back to the front door and then letting himself out into the street. He got into his car and drove himself home, laughing softly.

As for Arabella, blissfully unaware that she had been discovered, she gave her companions their suppers and went upstairs to clean and tidy up, then cooked her own meal before getting on with another cushion cover.

Saturday morning was busy. Dr Tavener, Miss Baird told her, had only two patients but he was going to the hospital and would probably not be back until after midday. 'So I'm afraid you won't be able to do your cleaning until he's gone again.'

Arabella, who turned the place upside-down on a Saturday, changed the flowers and polished everything possible, said she didn't mind. Secretly she was annoyed. She would have to do her weekly shopping and she didn't like to go out and leave him in his rooms—supposing the puppy were to bark? The shops closed at five o'clock—surely he wouldn't stay as late as that?

It was a relief when he came back just before everyone else went home, shut himself in his room for a while and then prepared to leave. Arabella was polishing the chairs in the waiting-room since Hoovering might disturb him and she heard him coming along the passage.

She had expected him to go straight to the door and let himself out but instead he stopped in the doorway, so she turned round to wish him good afternoon and found him staring at her. Her heart sank; he looked severe—surely he hadn't discovered about the puppy?

It seemed that he had. 'Since when have we had a dog in the house, Miss Lorimer?' His voice was silky and she didn't much care for it.

She put down her duster and faced him. 'He isn't a dog—he's a very small puppy.'

'Indeed? And have you Dr Marshall's permission to keep him here?'

'No. How did you know?'

'I saw him—and you—the other evening in the garden. I trust that he isn't rooting up the flowerbeds.'

She was suddenly fierce. 'If you'd been thrown in a gutter with your legs tied together and left to die you'd know what heaven it is to sniff the flowers.'

His mouth twitched. 'And you found him and of course brought him back with you?'

'Well, of course—and I cannot believe that, however ill-natured you are, you would have left him lying there.'

'You are quite right; I wouldn't. Perhaps if you could bear with my ill nature, I might take a look at him? He's probably in rather poor shape.'

'Oh, would you?' She paused on her way to the door. 'But you won't take him away and send him to a dogs' home? He's so very small.'

'No, I won't do that.'

She went ahead of him down the stairs and opened the basement door. Percy, asleep on the end of the bed, opened an eye and dozed off again but the puppy tumbled on to the floor and trotted towards them, waving his ridiculous tail.

Dr Tavener bent and scooped him up and tucked him under an arm.

'Very small,' he observed, 'and badly used too.' He was gently examining the little beast. 'One or two nasty sores on his flank . . .' He felt the small legs. 'How long have you had him?'

'Since last Saturday. I thought he was going to die.'

'You have undoubtedly saved his life. He needs a vet, though.' He looked at Arabella and smiled—a quite different man from the austere doctor who strode in and out of his consulting-room with barely a glance if they should meet—and she blinked with surprise.

'If I return at about four o'clock would you bring him to a vet with me? He is a friend of mine and will know if there is anything the little chap needs.'

Arabella goggled at him. 'Me? Go to the vet with you?'

'I don't bite,' said Dr Tavener mildly.

She went pink. 'I beg your pardon. I was only surprised. It's very kind of you. Only, please don't come before four o'clock because I've the week's shopping to do. It won't take long, will it? Percy likes his supper...'

'I don't imagine it will take too much time but you could leave—er—Percy's supper for him, couldn't you?'

'Well, yes.' She took the puppy from him. 'You're very kind.'

'In between bouts of ill nature,' he reminded her gently. Then watched the pretty colour in her cheeks. He went to the door. 'I will be back at four o'clock.'

Arabella crammed a lot into the next few hours. There was still the rubbish to take out to the dustbins outside and the brass on the front door to polish; she would see to those later, she told herself, changing into her decent suit and good shoes and doing her face and her hair. It was important to look as little like a caretaker as possible—she wouldn't want Dr Tavener to be ashamed of her. She took all the money she had with her, remembering the vet's bills for the dogs when her parents had been alive and, the picture of unassuming neatness, she went to the front door punctually at four o'clock.

He came in as she put her hand on the doorknob. He didn't waste time in civilities. 'Well? Where is the little beast?'

'In the basement. He's not allowed up here. I'll fetch him and bring him out to the car from my front door.'

'Do that. I'll be with you in a moment.' He went along to his rooms and she heard him phone as she went downstairs.

He was waiting by the car as she went through the door and up the steps with the puppy tucked under an arm and ushered her into the front seat, got in beside her and drove off.

The puppy was frightened and Arabella, concerned with keeping him quiet, hardly noticed where they were going. She looked up once and said, 'Oh, isn't that the Zoo?' and Dr Tavener grunted what she supposed to be yes. When he stopped finally and helped her out she looked around her with interest. She didn't know London very well—in happier days she and her mother had come up to shop or go to a theatre, and birthdays had been celebrated by her father taking them out to dine.

'Where is this?' she asked now.

'Little Venice. The vet lives in this house. His surgery is in the Marylebone Road but he agreed to see the puppy here.'

'That's very kind of him.' She went with him up the steps of the solid town house and, when the door was opened by a sober-looking woman in an apron, followed the doctor inside.

'He's expecting us, Mrs Wise,' said Dr Tavener easily. 'Are we to go up?'

'Yes, sir, you're expected.'

They were met at the head of the stairs by a man of the doctor's age, tall and thin, already almost bald.

'Come on in,' he greeted them. 'Where's this puppy, Titus?'

Dr Tavener stood aside so that Arabella came into view. 'This is Miss Arabella Lorimer—John Clarke, a wizard with animals.' He waited while they shook hands. 'Hand over the puppy, Miss Lorimer.'

They all went into a pleasant room, crowded with books and papers. There were two cats asleep on a chair and a black Labrador stretched out before a cheerful fire. 'Sit down,' invited Mr Clarke. 'I'll take a quick look.' He glanced at Arabella. 'Titus has told me about his rescue. At first glance I should imagine that good food and affection will soon put him on his feet.'

He bent over the little beast, examining him carefully and very gently. 'Nothing much wrong. I'll give you some stuff to put on those sores and I'll give him his injections while he's here. There's nothing broken or damaged, I'm glad to say. What's his name?'

'He hasn't got one yet.' She smiled at Mr Clarke, who smiled back.

'You can decide on that as you go home.' He handed the puppy back and she thanked him.

'Would you send the bill or shall I...?'

'Oh, I don't charge for emergencies or accidents,' said Mr Clarke cheerfully. 'Bring him for a check-up in a month or so—or earlier if you're worried. There will be a fee for that. Titus knows where the surgery is.'

'Thank you very much. I hope we haven't disturbed your Saturday afternoon.'

He flicked a glance at Dr Tavener's bland face. 'Not in the least. Nice to meet you and don't hesitate to get in touch if you are worried.'

Getting into the car again Arabella said, 'It was very kind of you, Dr Tavener, to bring us to the vet. Mr Clarke is a very nice man, isn't he? We've taken up a lot of your time. If you would drop us off at a bus stop we can go home...'

'Have you any idea which bus to catch?'

'Well, no, but I can ask.'

'I have a better idea. We will have tea and I will drive you back afterwards.'

'Have tea? Where? And really there is no need.'

'I said, "have tea", did I not? I live in the next street and my housekeeper will be waiting to make it. And don't fuss about Percy—we have been away for rather less than an hour and tea will take a fraction of that time.'

'The puppy?'

'Is entitled to his tea as well.' He had turned into a pleasant street bordering the canal and stopped before his house. 'Let us have no more questions!'

CHAPTER THREE

CLUTCHING the puppy, Arabella was swept into his house, one of several similar houses with their backs overlooking the canal and their fronts restrainedly Georgian. The hall was square with a curved staircase to one side and several doors leading from it. Out of one of these emerged a large, bony woman with a severe hairstyle and a long thin face.

'Ah, Alice. Miss Lorimer—this is my housekeeper, Mrs Turner. Alice, I've brought Miss Lorimer back for tea; could we have it presently?'

Arabella offered a hand and Mrs Turner shook it and said, 'How do you do?' in a severe manner and cast a look at the puppy. 'In five minutes, sir. And perhaps the young lady would like to leave her jacket.'

'No need,' he said cheerfully. 'She won't be staying long—it can stay on a chair.' He took the puppy as he spoke and Arabella took off her jacket and laid it tidily on a rather nice Regency elbow chair and went with him into the drawing-room.

It was large, running from front to back of the house, the back French windows opening on to a small wrought-iron balcony which overlooked the canal. She crossed the room, dimly aware of its beauty but intent on looking out of the window. 'It isn't like London at all,' she declared, 'and there's a garden...'

As indeed there was, below the balcony—small, high-walled, screened from the houses on either side by ornamental trees and shrubs, with the end wall built over the water.

Dr Tavener stood watching her and saying nothing and presently, aware of his silence, she turned to look at him. 'I'm sorry, I've been rude, but it was such a lovely surprise.'

He smiled then. 'Yes, isn't it? I've lived here for some years and it still surprises me. Come and sit down and we'll have tea.'

She looked around her then, at the comfortable chairs and the wide sofa before the fire; the Chippendale giltwood mirror over the fireplace and the rosewood table behind the sofa; the mahogany tripod tables with their lamps and the Dutch marquetry display cabinets each side of the fireplace. It was a beautiful room, furnished beautifully. There was a rosewood writing-table under the windows, its surface covered by silver-framed photos. She would have liked to have examined them but good manners forbade that so she sat down composedly in one of the armchairs as Mrs Turner came in with the tea tray.

Cucumber sandwiches, muffins in a silver dish and a rich fruit cake. She sighed silently and swallowed the lump in her throat; it was a long time since she had seen such a tea, eaten and drunk from fine china with the tea poured from a silver pot.

'Be mother,' invited the doctor, and sat down opposite her. He still had the puppy in his arms.

'Shall I have him?'

'No. No, he is no trouble. It is a pity that my own dog isn't here. She's a gentle creature—a golden Labrador—she would have mothered him.'

Arabella opened her mouth to ask him where she was and stopped just in time. Perhaps he would tell her. He didn't, but asked if he shouldn't be given a name.

She bit into a sandwich. 'Well, yes. Something rather grand, I thought, to make up for the beastly time he's had.'

'What a good idea. Have some of this cake—Mrs Turner is a good cook.' He smiled a little. 'But I'm talking to one, aren't I?'

She wasn't sure about the smile—perhaps he was being a bit sarcastic.

'What kind of a dog is he?'

'Rather mixed, I fancy; the ears are very like a spaniel's and I imagine he will grow to some considerable size—look at his paws. I'm not sure about that tail. As to the name . . . how about Bassett?'

She gave him a thoughtful look and then laughed. 'Of course—how clever you are. Bassett's Allsorts!'

When she laughed she looked almost pretty, he decided. It would be interesting to find out more about her; when she forgot to be the caretaker she was someone quite different.

However, she hadn't forgotten. She put down her cup and got to her feet. 'I've stayed longer than I intended. I hope I haven't spoilt your afternoon, sir.'

He didn't try to keep her but fetched her jacket and settled her with Bassett in the car, making pleasant conversation as he did so. He went with her into the rooms at Wigmore Street when they arrived, checking that everything was as it should be, before bidding her a coolly friendly good evening and opening the door. He was closing it behind him when she cried, 'Stop, oh, do stop. Must I tell Dr Marshall about Bassett?'

'Of course. On Monday morning before his patients come.' He stared down at her troubled face. 'I will have a word with him first—he is a very kind man and besides, you are a very good caretaker.'

'Oh, will you? You promise? You won't forget?'

His eyes were cold. 'I keep my promises, Miss Lorimer, and I have an excellent memory.'

'Oh dear, I've annoyed you.'

'No, you don't annoy me; you surprise me, vex me and intrigue me, but that is all.' He nodded and this time the door closed firmly behind him, leaving her in the hall, her thoughts in a fine muddle.

She had forgotten to thank him for her tea too. She went down to her room and attended to the animals' wants and then went back to finish her cleaning. Tomorrow, if it was fine enough, she would take Bassett for a walk—Regent's Park wasn't too far away. She would have to carry him, of course, for she had no lead and he had no collar. She dismissed Dr Tavener from her thoughts. He had been kind and helpful but he didn't like her—worse, she doubted if he had formed any opinion of her at all. She was of no interest to him whatsoever, although he was prepared to help her if necessary—just as he would help a stranger who had stumbled in the street, or an old lady to cross a road. It was mortifying but it made sense.

She enjoyed her Sunday, walking briskly in the park with Bassett tucked under her arm and going back to her dinner—lamp chop, potato purée, sprouts and carrots cooked with sugar and butter. The three of them ate their meal and settled down for the afternoon before tea by the fire. Really a very pleasant day, decided Arabella, getting ready for bed later, and she was so lucky to have a home of her own and a job. She had managed all day to forget about seeing Dr Marshall in the morning but she woke in the night and worried about it, dropping off again at last with the thought that Dr Tavener had said he would have a word. 'I dare say,' she said, addressing the sleeping animals, 'he is a very nice man under that distant manner. If I knew him better I might even like him.'

Dr Tavener, driving himself home in the early hours of the morning after an urgent summons to a patient's bedside, was thinking about her too. He had telephoned Dr Marshall and told him about Bassett, and James Marshall, good-natured and amused, had agreed to allow the puppy to stay.

They had laughed about it together but now, driving through the silent streets, his thoughts were more serious. Arabella was a nice girl; she shouldn't be a caretaker in the first place. She might have no qualifications but she came from a good background; he remembered the nicely laid table when he had had his supper with her and her unselfconscious assurance at his house that afternoon. This wasn't her kind of life at all but he could see no way of bettering it. Finding something more suited to her would be difficult because of the cat and puppy and he knew enough about her to realise that she would never give them up.

He let himself into his house and Beauty, whom he had fetched that afternoon, came to meet him and went with him to the kitchen while he made himself a cup of coffee.

He sat, a tired man, drinking it with her at his feet. 'The answer is to find her a husband,' he told her. Beauty thumped her tail and he rubbed her ears gently,

saw her into her basket and went back upstairs to his
bed—there were still two or three hours before he
needed to get up. His last thought before he slept was
that finding exactly the right man for Arabella would
be a difficult task.

Arabella, very neat in her overall, presented herself
at Dr Marshall's desk as soon as he was sitting at it.
His good morning was kindly. 'Problems?' he wanted
to know.

She didn't beat about the bush, but she didn't
mention Dr Tavener either. He might have forgotten
to speak to Dr Marshall and that might be awkward.
He hadn't forgotten. Dr Marshall smiled at her. 'Ah,
yes, Titus tells me that we have acquired a dog.
Splendid, I have no objection just as long as you don't
let him loose on our patients. Quite comfortable, are
you? Settled in now?'

She could have flung her arms round his neck. 'Yes,
thank you, sir.'

'Run along, then, the doorbell will be ringing at
any moment now.'

As she was leaving he stopped her. 'I think it would
be more suitable if we called you Arabella. You have
no objection?'

'No, sir.' They could call her anything they liked;
Bassett was hers.

She was admitting a patient when Dr Tavener arrived, nodded a good morning and went straight to
his room. The next patient to arrive was for him—a
tall, good-looking girl, dressed expensively and skil-
fully made-up.

No one bothered to give Arabella more than a
fleeting glance and sometimes a vague smile of thanks

and she was about to do the same but stopped short. 'Arabella—whatever are you doing here? Good gracious—that frightful overall and your hair all screwed up.'

Arabella closed the door. 'Hello, Daphne. I work here. You're here to see Dr Tavener? He's down the hall...'

Daphne laughed. 'Oh, my dear, I know where he is—we're old friends. But what do you do exactly?'

'I'm the caretaker.'

Daphne pealed with laughter. 'My goodness, what a marvellous joke.' She would have said more but the doorbell was rung again and Arabella went to answer it. When she turned round Daphne was gone.

Presently, ushered into Dr Tavener's room, Daphne sat down opposite his desk. 'Hello, Titus. It's ages since we saw you—Mother was asking what had happened to you. I'm not ill but I do wish you'd give me something for my headaches.' She crossed an elegant leg. 'I've had such a surprise—Arabella, a girl I know, opened the door. She said she was the caretaker, of all things! A caretaker—I ask you. I expect you know she was left penniless when her parents were killed some months ago. A bit of a come-down from living in comfort. Not a great friend, of course,' she laughed. 'We lived some miles away from each other but we had mutual friends...' She smiled charmingly. 'Now, what about my headaches...?'

He had sat quietly while she talked, now he said blandly, 'You tell me where the pain is exactly. Perhaps you are worried about something or doing too much?'

'Parties, you mean? Well, I do enjoy life—why not? We're only young once and besides, it helps one from getting bored.'

'The boredom probably accounts for the headaches. I suggest that you miss a few late nights and take a long walk every day. Cut down on the drinks and go to bed at a reasonable time.'

She pouted prettily. 'Oh, Titus, you stuffy old thing! And I was going to invite you to come home for the weekend but now I shan't.'

'I'm not free in any case,' he told her blandly. He stood up and handed her the prescription he had written. 'Take these for a week and see how you get on. If you're no better we'll delve deeper. I'm sure it's nothing for you to worry about.'

He held the door open for her and she smiled up at him as she went past. A lovely face, he reflected, but nothing behind it. If he was to marry it would have to be a woman of intelligence, who would listen to him without twiddling her earrings or examining her nails. She had no need to be beautiful or even pretty—the right clothes would take care of that... It was only recently that he had wished for a companion. He was, he considered, past the age of falling in love and besides, a marriage founded on liking and compatibility was more likely to succeed than one plunged into in the heat of the moment.

He sat down at his desk, dismissing the matter from his mind, and picked up the next patient's notes.

His day's work done, his thoughts reverted to Arabella. It was unthinkable that she should remain as a caretaker—polishing and Hoovering and cleaning windows and doors, dragging out the rubbish to be collected, polishing the brass and, above all, being alone at night with no protection save that of a very small puppy and a cat. The matter needed urgent consideration.

As for Arabella, she avoided him as much as possible while at the same time wishing that she knew more about him. The small glimpse she had had of his life had intrigued her. She had supposed him to be a dyed-in-the-wool bachelor but, listening from time to time to the nurses gossiping, she had formed the opinion that he was much sought-after socially—a matrimonial prize several women were after. Hadn't she seen with her own eyes how her erstwhile friend Daphne had smiled up at him? She thought that it might be rather nice to be married to someone like him, to live in a lovely house and meet people again. To have clothes—new clothes, bought without having to look at the price-ticket first. That, she told herself, was no reason for marrying. She finished tidying the rooms and went downstairs to get her supper and take the animals for their evening stroll in the garden.

Saturday came round once more. Arabella did her shopping, gave the rooms their usual turn-out and went into the garden to pick some fresh flowers. Bassett had filled out and lost most of his timidity and followed Percy's dignified progress from one flowerbed to the other. Tomorrow, she promised him, he would wear his new collar and walk beside her on his lead in the park.

The evenings were getting colder; they all went indoors presently and had their suppers and then shared the warmth of the gas fire. The cushion covers were finished so she had brought some of the magazines

down from the waiting-room and curled up to read
them.

Before going to bed she went back upstairs once
more to check that everything was closed and locked.
The upstairs flat was empty again but she had grown
used to being on her own.

She enjoyed every minute of Sunday. The walk in
the park had been a great success; Bassett had be-
haved well, trotting along on his lead, chasing the
fallen leaves and barking his small treble bark. They
had gone back to Percy's welcome and had their tea
and afterwards she sat down and did her sums for the
week.

Even with three mouths to feed she was saving a
little money each week. The future was uncertain; even
if she stayed with the doctors for the rest of her
working life, she would still need money when she
retired. It seemed a long way ahead, but she might be
ill, lose her job, need a home while she found something else. In a month or two, when she felt more
secure, she would start looking for a post as a cook.
Surely there was somewhere and someone who
wouldn't object to a cat and a dog? It was going to
be difficult and she was happy enough in her basement
but she was aware that both the doctors felt an un-
easiness about her working for them. She suspected
that Dr Marshall had given her her job on a sudden
whim and while he might not be regretting it he could
be having second thoughts...

She finished the sums, gave Percy and Bassett their
suppers and went into the garden with them and, once
indoors again, bolted the door before beginning to
get her own supper. That eaten, she decided to check

the rooms upstairs and go to bed early. Life, she decided, though dull, was at least secure.

Before she slept she allowed herself to daydream a
little. Being a practical girl, she didn't allow her
thoughts to dwell on the prospect of some young man
falling head over heels in love with her and marrying
her out of hand, but on the miraculous offer of a job
as cook—a highly paid job in some stately home—
with a cottage in the grounds and no objection to
pets...

The partners had arrived early on the Monday
morning and Dr Marshall had wandered along to Dr
Tavener's rooms. 'Nice morning,' he observed af-
fably. 'The garden looks pretty good too.' He glanced
at the small chrysanths arranged on the desk. 'Keeps
the place looking nice, does our Arabella.'

Dr Tavener had been writing; now he put down his
pen. 'James, we shall have to do something about her.
We ought never to have given her the job in the first
place. I had a patient the other morning—she had
been at school with Arabella, known her for years,
saw a lot of her before the parents were killed.'

'And this friend, was she shocked at Arabella
working in such a lowly capacity?'

Dr Tavener frowned. 'I believe she was rather
amused...'

'Hardly a friend. I imagine Arabella is very proud,
not wishing to be an embarrassment to her friends,
going it alone.'

Dr Tavener said deliberately, 'I don't like the idea
of her being alone here at night.'

His partner peered at him through his specs. 'No? Perhaps you are right; she's rather small although not at all nervous, she told me.'

'She would have said anything to get a roof over her head.'

'So what are we to do about it? Other than finding her a husband...'

'She is a cordon bleu cook. If we could find someone who would accept those animals she would be safe and secure and living in surroundings more suited to her.'

'Until she finds a husband. She would make a good wife and a handy one too—no need to call out the plumber or the electrician. Come to think of it, Titus, she would suit you very well and it's time you had a wife—patients like a married man!'

Titus didn't answer and Dr Marshall said hastily, 'Only joking. Time I went back, I suppose. Are you fully booked this morning?'

'Yes, and this afternoon. I've a clinic this evening.'

'You must come to dinner soon—I'll get Angie to phone you.'

'I'd like that, thanks.'

Dr Tavener opened the case sheets before him but made no effort to read them. That was the solution, he decided: to find a job for Arabella. In the country—because she was a country girl at heart. The place would be very empty without her, though.

Arabella, unaware of the future being planned for her, went about her chores, bought some wool going cheap because of the colour—a serviceable brown which wasn't selling well—and started on a sweater, keeping a loving eye on Percy and Bassett.

* * *

Dr Tavener, a man of considerable wealth, owned a
pleasant small manor house in Wiltshire which had
been in the family for more than two hundred years.
Whenever his work permitted he drove himself back
there, taking Beauty with him, spending his days gar-
dening and walking. His parents were dead but his
grandmother lived there with a meek companion,
looked after by Butter and his wife who had also
looked after his mother and father and probably, if
they lived long enough, would look after him in his
old age. He couldn't imagine the place without them.

He went there the following weekend, on a blustery
autumn day. Twenty miles or so beyond Swindon he
turned off the motorway to take a minor road towards Tetbury. Then, turning off again, took a narrow
lane which brought him eventually to a small village
and, beyond it, to his home.

There were lights in the windows and smoke coming
from several of its elaborate brick chimney-pots, and
as he stopped before the door it opened to allow a
dog to rush out and race to the car, barking happily.
Beauty's brother, Duke. He circled the car, delighted
to see its occupants, and the three of them went indoors to where Butter was waiting.

'Good to see you again, Master Titus,' said Butter.
'Mrs Butter has tea all ready and waiting. I'll take the
dogs along to the kitchen for their meal. Mrs Tavener
is in the drawing room.'

Dr Tavener crossed the polished wood floor of the
hall and went into the room—long and low-ceilinged,
its strapwork still perfect, with windows at either end
of it—lattice windows set in square bays—and the
heavy velvet curtains blending with the dark green and
russet of the vast carpet.

It was furnished with a clever mixture of Jacobean and early Georgian chairs and tables and the fireplace was of the Queen Anne period—ornate and heavily ornamented with a vast mirror above it. On either side of it there were comfortable armchairs and a great sofa but the two ladies in the room were sitting in upright Regency armchairs with a small table between them upon which lay playing cards.

Dr Tavener crossed the room and bent to kiss his grandmother—a handsome old lady, sitting very upright, her features severe. She smiled as he greeted her. 'Titus, my dear, how pleasant to see you again. You don't come home enough.'

'My home is in London,' he pointed out mildly. 'At least while I'm working.'

'Yes, yes and I'm sure it is a very handsome house, but this is the family home.' She paused. 'It is time you had a family, Titus.'

He only smiled and went to shake her companion's hand. Miss Welling was a thin lady of uncertain age with a sharp nose, myopic brown eyes and an anxious expression. There was no need for the anxiety—she received nothing but kindness and consideration from her employer—but meekness and anxiety seemed to be her nature and old Mrs Tavener might look severe but she would never tax her with questions and over the years had come to accept Miss Welling's cautious approach to life.

Miss Welling greeted Dr Tavener in a pleased voice, for she liked him, then excused herself with the plea that she would see if the tea tray was ready and slid out of the room.

'The dear creature,' said Mrs Tavener, 'anyone would think that I beat her. Come and sit down and tell me what you have been doing lately.'

He drew up a chair and embarked on a brief account of his days. The tea was brought in presently and afterwards he took the dogs for a walk in the deepening twilight. When he returned it was to find his grandmother alone. 'Miss Welling has gone to tidy herself, my dear. We have half an hour to ourselves— time in which to tell me what is on your mind.'

When he gave her a half-smiling look she said, 'You are very like your father—the bigger the problem, the more bland the face. Fallen in love at last?'

'No. No, I believe that I shall never do that seriously enough to marry. But I do have a problem...' He told her about Arabella, his voice placid and disinterested, and when he had finished he asked, 'Have you any ideas, Grandmother?'

'The young woman seems to be in most unsuitable work. On the other hand, Titus, she has a home of sorts, independence and is able to keep her pets with her. A sense of security must be very important to her—to be pitched out without warning into poverty and loneliness must have been such a shock. To subject her to an unknown future seems unkind, even if the work was more congenial, and who knows if she would be happy? Besides, you would lose touch with her. You like her?'

'Yes, I do. Surprisingly we have a good deal in common; she is undemanding as a companion and not above treating me with a tart tongue.'

Mrs Tavener hid a smile. 'She sounds as though she is very well able to look after herself, although I do agree with you that being in that place alone at night isn't quite the thing.' She glanced at him. 'But I will ask around, my dear, and if I hear of anything at all suitable I will let you know at once. The girl's presentable?'

'Yes—good clothes but out of date, nice manners, no looks to speak of but nice eyes—beautiful eyes—and a pleasant voice.'

Mrs Tavener considered this reply and decided not to comment upon it. Instead she said, 'I shall be coming up to town next week to shop. Will you give us beds for the night? Miss Welling will come with me, of course, but I promise you we will be no trouble to you.'

'That will be delightful. Would you like to go to the theatre? There are some good plays on. I'm afraid I shall be away from home all day but I can make sure I'm free in the evenings.'

'A play would be most enjoyable. Something romantic with music if possible. Will three days be too much for you?'

'Make it longer if you wish, Grandmother. You know you're always more than welcome.'

'Yes, my dear, I do know. We will come up on the Tuesday and return here on Thursday evening. Butter shall drive us up and fetch us again.' She paused. 'There's no reason why Mrs Butter shouldn't come up with him, then they could drive up early in the morning and she could go to the shops for an hour or two before he picks us up.'

'A good idea. Make any arrangements you like with Mrs Turner.'

'Thank you. Would it bother you to take a look at Miss Welling while we're there? She can go along to your rooms—I'll put her in a taxi. She won't admit it but I don't think she sleeps very well.'

'Yes, of course. I'll get Miss Baird to make an appointment and phone you.'

Miss Welling came into the room and they talked of other things.

He took the old lady to church on Sunday morning and after lunch spent the rest of the day reading the Sunday papers, taking the dogs for a walk, having his tea and then driving himself back to his house in Little Venice. He made a detour when he reached town so that he could drive along Wigmore Street. The basement curtains were closed but there was a fringe of light showing round them and he stifled the urge to knock at the door and spend an hour with Arabella, telling her about his weekend. 'Ridiculous,' he told himself sharply so that Beauty, sitting beside him half-asleep, gave a sleepy bark.

Mrs Tavener was driven up to London on Tuesday and by the time Dr Tavener got home that evening she was settled in, sitting in his drawing-room playing Racing Demon with Miss Welling. They spent a pleasant evening together and he told her that he had got tickets for a long-running musical which he hoped that she would like. He had seen it himself in the company of an old friend's daughter who had been visiting in London. He hadn't liked the show particularly but perhaps that was because he had found his companion a singularly vapid girl with no conversation who was everlastingly fidgeting with her hair or her lipstick.

As for Miss Welling, she was to see him the next morning despite her timid objections that he was a busy man and she was perfectly well. 'Well, of course you are,' he had told her kindly, 'but since you are here it is a splendid opportunity to have a check-up. It won't take too long and I'll put you in a taxi afterwards so that you can come straight back here.'

Arabella, checking Miss Baird's list of patients, noticed that Dr Tavener had added a name at the end of Miss Baird's list. A Miss Welling—and not until eleven o'clock. Usually on Wednesday he left soon after ten o'clock to take an outpatients clinic at one of the hospitals. She had seen him only briefly on Monday and Tuesday and he had acknowledged her good morning with a brisk nod; she would try to avoid him in future since he seemed to dislike her so much. She puzzled over that, for he had been kind about Bassett and when she had had tea with him he had been so friendly that she had quite forgotten that she was his caretaker...

Wednesday morning was dark and cold and drizzling with rain, and those patients she admitted were short-tempered as a result. To her pleasant good morning they either grunted or let loose a string of complaints while they shook umbrellas over her pleasingly polished floor or hung their damp raincoats over her arms. It was a bit depressing, so when the bell rang once again and she opened the door it was a pleasant surprise to be greeted cheerfully by the elderly lady wishing to enter. She was accompanied by a lady considerably younger with a woebegone face who none the less answered Arabella's cheerful greeting with a smile.

'Miss Welling? If you would see the receptionist and then go down the passage to Dr Tavener's waiting-room. Shall I take your coat?'

The elderly lady gave her companion a poke in the ribs. 'Yes, go along, do. I'll be in the waiting-room.'

She turned to Arabella. 'A wretched day, is it not? London can be horrid in this weather. You live here, I expect?'

'Oh, yes. I'm the caretaker. Would you like me to have your coat too?'

'No. No, thank you. You don't look very much like a caretaker.'

Arabella blushed but the lady was old and perhaps she was just being inquisitive. 'I'm very content; it's a good job. Shall I show you to Dr Tavener's waiting-room?'

'By all means, and here is Miss Welling back again. Good day to you.'

Mrs Tavener swept away with Miss Welling at her heels and Arabella went downstairs. Miss Welling was the last patient; she would have a quick cup of coffee before seeing her out presently.

Miss Welling, emerging from Dr Tavener's consulting-room some twenty minutes later, was accompanied by him to the door. 'I'll arrange a taxi——' He broke off at the sight of his grandmother sitting very erect in the waiting-room. Her 'Good morning, Titus,' was graciously said but she smiled as she spoke.

He said nothing for the moment but smiled a little in his turn before crossing the room and taking her hand. 'What do you think of her?' he asked. 'For that is why you are here, is it not?'

'Of course, you are quite right, Titus, she is most unsuitable. You will have to think of something else. As you said, she is quite without good looks. Although, of course, good looks don't matter if one is a good cook.' She stood up. 'Did you find Miss Welling in good health?'

'On the whole, yes. May we discuss that this evening? I'm late for my clinic.'

His nurse was in the examination room so he saw the two ladies to the door and a few minutes later left himself, so that when Arabella came upstairs again there was only his nurse there, grumbling because he intended to come back that afternoon and she had hoped to be free to go home early.

Arabella, nipping through the rain to the shops, reflected that Dr Tavener probably worked too hard. She hoped that he had time to eat proper meals and had enough sleep. It was difficult to tell because he was always beautifully turned out and he had the kind of face which gave away nothing of his feelings.

Choosing carrots and turnips with a careful eye, she reminded herself to stop thinking about him—it was such a waste of time.

CHAPTER FOUR

DR TAVENER did not know when the preposterous idea first entered his head. Perhaps at a dinner party as he sat with a charming woman on either side of him, both looking for a husband and both divorced. Not a conceited man, he was aware all the same that he had good looks, a splendid physique and more than enough money to satisfy the greediest of women. Or it might have been one early morning, when he had gone to his manor for a weekend and taken the dogs out into the garden before breakfast. It had been a cold night and the frost had iced every blade of grass and twig and he had wanted Arabella there beside him to enjoy it too. 'Not that I am in love with her,' he had told Beauty. 'It is merely that she is a good companion.' She would stand between him and the tiresome women who were introduced to him by his friends in the mistaken idea that he might like to make one of them his wife. She would be restful to come home to...

Because the idea was so preposterous, he avoided her as much as possible. Arabella wondered what she had done to annoy him, for if they did meet the look he cast at her was thunderous. It made her unhappy, for he had been kind, and from time to time had smoothed her path. She did her best to forget it.

It was in the middle of the week, in the morning while she was still getting the rooms ready for the day, that the electricity failed. A fuse probably, she thought, and since it was still dark groped her way to the hall where she had had the forethought to put a torch in the table drawer.

The electrics were in a cupboard at the back of the hall. She peered inside, saw what had to be done and, since the fuses were in a box tucked away behind everything else, she got down on her knees the better to get at them.

Dr Tavener, arriving early, had come in silently and stopped short at the sight of Arabella's shapely person sticking out of the cupboard but before he could speak she had crawled out backwards and got to her feet, clutching the new fuse. She spoke tartly. 'Well, you might have rung the bell or something—I might have known it would be you.'

She wiped a dirty hand over a cheek and left a smudge.

'How did you know that it was I?'

'Your feet . . .'

'My feet?' He had put down the bag and taken the fuse from her.

She went a little pink. 'Well, I get to know the sound of people's feet.'

He nodded and went past her, fixed the fuse, and came back to where she had resumed Hoovering. She switched off to thank him and when she would have switched on again he put out a hand and stopped her. 'A moment, Arabella. There is something I wish to say to you. Unfortunately there is not time to explain fully but I should like to make you a proposal.'

At her look of astonishment he added kindly. 'Don't look so surprised. I should like you to consider marrying me. If you will think about it we can discuss it sensibly at a later date.'

He smiled then. 'Don't let me keep you from your work.' He had gone into his room and shut the door quietly behind him, leaving her with her mouth open, a white face and a rapid pulse.

As for Dr Tavener, he sat down at his desk and wondered if he had gone mad.

Arabella had no doubts about it—he had been overworking and had had a brainstorm, whatever that was, and hadn't known what he was saying. She would ignore the whole thing, let him see that she hadn't taken him seriously.

The last patient had gone by five o'clock that afternoon and everyone else followed him within half an hour. Arabella collected her cleaning things and went upstairs to tidy up. She had finished and was tying up the plastic bag of rubbish when Dr Tavener returned.

He had a bottle under one arm and a box with a Harrods label in his hand. 'May I come to supper? You can't leave the place, otherwise I would have given you dinner at home.'

She put the sack down. 'Look, I do understand. I expect you've been working too hard and thought you were talking to someone else. It doesn't matter a bit...'

He took the sack from her. 'No, you don't understand and I'm perfectly sound in my head. Shall we have supper and talk?' He smiled suddenly and she found herself smiling back. 'I have a great deal to explain.'

'Very well.' She led the way downstairs and he took the sack outside to the refuse bins, giving her the bottle and the box to hold. He hadn't been mad at all, he reflected, washing his hands at the sink—this was going to be one of the sanest things he had ever done.

Arabella peered into her small pantry. She had decided to have an egg and a baked potato for her supper but that wouldn't do for her guest. She measured macaroni and put it on to cook, grated cheese and beat an egg, scrubbed two more potatoes and put them in the oven and all the while he sat with Percy on his knee and Bassett curled up on his shoes, saying nothing. It was unnerving. She thought of several things to say but none of them seemed suitable. She held her tongue and laid the table.

He had brought a bottle of claret with him this time. He uncorked it and left it to breathe and presently he poured it and gave her a glass.

She sipped. 'Delicious,' she said. 'What's in the box?'

'Fruit pies. Can you sit down for a while or must you stay by the stove?'

She had put the macaroni cheese in the oven—it and the potatoes would be another half-hour and there was only a lettuce to dress.

She sat in the armchair and he took a chair from beside the table and sat opposite her. 'I appreciate the fact that I must have taken you by surprise but I do assure you that I was serious.' When she would have spoken he went on, 'No, please, let me explain. I am forty years old, Arabella—not a young man. I have been in and out of love on numerous occasions but I have never found the right woman and so I preferred to stay single. Lately, however, I have wished for a wife, someone to come home to each day, a companion for my leisure and someone who would put an end to my well-meaning friends vying with each other to marry me off to a succession of suitable young women. You see that I wish to marry for the wrong reasons, although perhaps they are no worse than many others. However, those are my reasons. I like you too much to pretend there are others. I am not in love with you and yet I enjoy your company so much that I have begun to miss you when you are not here. It worries me that you are living here alone, doing menial work, and having no friends or fun. We could get along very well together, I think, Arabella, to our mutual advantage.'

Arabella said quietly, 'This isn't...? That is, you are not suggesting this out of pity? Because if you are I shall probably throw something at you.'

She had, she reflected, had several proposals in happier times, but never one as forthright and un-sentimental as this one.

Dr Tavener gave her an austere look. 'I do not pity you—never have pitied you. You interest me, fre-quently annoy me, amuse me, agree with me over the things which matter.'

'You're very outspoken...'

'Would you have me otherwise? Would you have believed me if I had told you that I was in love with you?'

'Of course not! The idea's absurd.' Her nose twitched. 'Supper's ready.'

She liked him for getting up at once to pour more wine and carry the plates to the table, talking now of a variety of matters and never once speaking of them-selves. It gave her time to get over the shock.

They ate the macaroni cheese and potatoes and salad, and the fruit pies, all the while carrying on an unforced conversation—arguing about books, disagreeing amicably over the right cultivation of roses, agreeing about the pleasures of having animals to look after. 'I had a pony,' said Arabella wistfully, 'and a donkey.' She paused.

'And?' said Dr Tavener quietly.

'They wanted to sell them, but I took them to an animal sanctuary. They are still there, I hope. I simply hated leaving them.'

'Somewhere near your home?'

'Oh, yes. You must have heard of it.'

When she told him the name he nodded. 'I have heard of it. They have a fine reputation.'

She made coffee presently, while he washed up. He made a good job of it so she asked him if he looked after himself. 'Although you have a housekeeper, haven't you?'

'Mrs Turner took me in hand when my parents died. I admit that I seldom need to do household chores but I'm perfectly able to do so if need be.'

They took their coffee to drink by the fire and the animals pushed and shoved each other as near its warmth as possible.

Arabella took a sip of coffee. She had drunk too much wine and it had gone to her head. It had given her a pretty colour too. She was aware of Dr Tavener's eyes searching her face and buried her nose in her mug.

'Well——' he sounded brisk '—how long to you need to make up your mind?'

'I think,' said Arabella carefully, 'that I won't be able to make it up until I'm alone. You see, while you are here, you distract me.' She added hastily, 'That sounds rude but I don't mean to be; it's just that I

have to think about it from a distance, if you see what
I mean.'

'Yes, I see. You may have a week, Arabella, and
then I shall ask you again. During that week I shall
take no notice of you at all—not because I wish to
avoid you but so that you can decide for yourself.'

He got up and drew her to her feet, holding her
hands between his. They felt cool and comforting and
undemanding. 'Thank you for my supper.' He bent
and kissed her cheek. 'Goodnight, Arabella.'

She stared up into his faintly smiling face. 'But you
might have second thoughts...'

'No, I can promise that I won't.' He went to the
door. 'No need to come up, I'll lock the door after
me—but remember to bolt it after me later, won't
you?'

She sat for a long time doing nothing, her head in
a turmoil, but it was no good thinking about it any
more. In the morning she would be able to reflect upon
her surprising evening with her usual good sense.

She went upstairs and bolted the door and checked
the place as she always did and then went back to
shower and go to her bed. 'I shan't sleep,' she told
Percy, already perched on the end of the bed and
giving Bassett a thorough wash. And she slept as soon
as her head was on the pillow.

In the half light of a dull November morning the
whole thing seemed like an impossible dream. By the
end of a busy day peopled by ill-tempered patients, a
crusty Dr Marshall and only glimpses of Dr Tavener's
broad back it didn't seem quite as impossible.

She was unable to make up her mind. She had
argued, with Percy and Bassett as a more or less at-
tentive audience, each evening, weighing up the pros

and cons. But however matter-of-factly she put her problems it wasn't the same as talking to someone. With the end of the week looming she decided that something would have to be done. As Dr Tavener, last as usual, left that evening she stopped him as he went to the door.

'Could you spare five minutes? I need someone to talk to and ask advice, only I don't know anyone except you. I wondered if you would mind. It's about us, but if we could pretend that we're discussing two other people, if you see what I mean . . .'

'A sensible suggestion. Come into my room and we will see what can be done.'

She was relieved to hear nothing but a pleasantly detached voice and accompanied him back to his consulting-room, where he threw his overcoat on to a chair, offered her a seat and went to sit at his desk once more. Arabella, momentarily diverted by the thought that the overcoat—a splendid one of cashmere—should have been hung up properly and not cast in a heap, gathered her wandering thoughts and faced him.

'It's like this,' she explained. 'I—that is, the girl I'm asking you about isn't sure that she would be doing the right thing if she married this man. She doesn't know what will be expected of her. Does he go out a great deal? Would his friends like her? Perhaps she wouldn't like them. She wouldn't want to shame him; she's not clever or witty or anything like that. She might make a mess of the whole thing, and the thing is she's out of date about getting divorced and all that——' She eyed him with a severe look across the desk. 'If you're married, you do your best to make a success of it.'

She was watching his face and seeing nothing but placid interest there.

His voice was quiet. 'The girl is worrying need-lessly. She has, if I might say so, too small an opinion of herself. She is perfectly able to fulfil the duties of a professional man's wife. She would be surprised how tiring clever and witty women are after a hard day's work and a marriage undertaken in mutual liking and respect is unlikely to come to grief. Indeed, the fact that there are no strong feelings involved should ensure its success.' He smiled at her. 'Does that help?'

She nodded. 'Yes. I think so. There's one other thing, though. You're rich.'

He said apologetically, 'I'm afraid I am, rather, but I have never let it bother me, nor would I allow it to bother you.'

'No—well, you see, I wouldn't marry you for your money.'

'No, no, I'm sure you wouldn't.' He spoke gravely; she didn't see the gleam of amusement in his eyes.

She got up. 'Thank you for letting me talk and for giving me advice. I hope I haven't made you late for anything.'

He assured her that she hadn't, bade her a cheerful goodnight and took himself off home where Mrs Turner met him with the warning that he would be late for his dinner engagement with the Marshalls. 'Forgot the time, I suppose,' she observed. 'Head buried in your books as like as not.' She went back to her kitchen saying over her shoulder, 'Time you were married, Doctor. And if I've said that once, I've said it a hundred times!'

He laughed as he went up the stairs two at a time. 'One day I'll surprise you,' he promised her.

*   *   *

'I told you to come early, Titus,' complained Angie Marshall as he offered apologies and an armful of roses.

'Got held up?' asked Dr Marshall easily. 'Come in and have a drink. There's no one else coming so we can talk shop if we want to. You'll come to Angie's dinner party at Christmas, won't you? She's rooting round for a suitable young woman to capture your attention.' He didn't wait for a reply. 'We had a busy day. Stayed behind to catch up on the paperwork?'

'No.' Titus had sat down opposite his host and hostess in the comfortable drawing-room. 'I had a talk with Arabella.'

'Nice little thing. Worried about something, is she?' He glanced at his wife. 'You'd like her, Angie. A pity you can't find her a good husband.'

'No need. She's going to marry me,' said Dr Tavener.

'Bless my soul! She's exactly right for you, Titus. You should have brought her along with you this evening.'

'I left her Hoovering and muttering about dripping taps.'

Mrs Marshall laughed. 'Titus, she sounds a dear and just your sort. Not in the least sentimental, and practical as well. Is she very in love with you?'

He answered calmly. 'Not in the least. Nor I with her, but we like each other and agree about everything which we consider important. I have every expectation that our marriage will be an enduring success.'

'We've known you for a long time—years and years,' said Mrs Marshall, 'and I was beginning to think that you would never marry. We're so happy for you both, Titus.' She added, 'She will be nice to come home to, my dear.'

He smiled. 'Angie, what an understanding woman you are. A good thing James appreciates you.'

'We've been married for sixteen years.' Dr Marshall sounded smug. 'Bring Arabella here for dinner and let her see how successful marriage can be.' He added, 'Oh, lord, we'll have to find another caretaker.'

'How about the ex-bus driver?'

'A good idea. I'll get Miss Baird on to it first thing in the morning.'

The three of them spent the rest of the evening in undemanding talk and later the two men went to Dr Marshall's study to discuss their various patients. It was late when Dr Tavener arrived back at his house; Mrs Turner had gone to bed. He put the car away in the mews garage and took Beauty for a walk through the quiet streets, feeling content.

Arabella was content too. Her mind was made up and she had no intention of altering it. She had seen enough sad results from friends who had married in a blaze of romance and come to grief within a few years to know that liking the same things—books, music, a way of living—as well as pleasure in each other's company were more likely to last even if they lacked excitement. Of course, she admitted to herself, being in love would be marvellous too, but it was obvious to her that Dr Tavener wasn't a man to waste time over romance and, since both of them had nothing but liking for each other, she could see no reason why their marriage shouldn't succeed.

True to his word, Dr Tavener made no attempt to speak to her, the weekend came and went, and suddenly the week was up.

Everyone but the two doctors had gone home. They stood in the hall talking; Arabella could hear them as she collected her cleaning things from under the stairs. Perhaps he wouldn't come—perhaps he expected her to go upstairs... She heard Dr Marshall laugh and the front door bang shut and a moment later Dr Tavener came down the stairs. He took her broom and dusters from her and ushered her back into the room. 'Never mind that now,' she was told briskly. 'Will you marry me, Arabella?'

He could have been asking her to post a letter for all the emotion in his voice. But what else had she expected? She sat down and waved him to a chair. She said, 'Yes,' and, since that sounded a bit terse, added, 'Yes, thank you. I will.'

'Splendid. We can go ahead with our plans. You can leave here at the end of this week—there's a caretaker lined up to start on Sunday. I'll get a special license—James Marshall will give you away—we can be married quietly...'

She said tartly, 'You said our plans—you seem to have taken it for granted that I would agree to everything you have arranged.'

'I'm sorry—oh, I'm sorry! That was unforgivable of me. All this week I have been planning and plotting. Say what you wish to do, Arabella, and you shall have your way.'

She said seriously, 'Well, actually, it all sounds very sensible. Where am I to go?'

'I have a house in the country—in a village midway between Tetbury and Malmsbury. My grandmother lives there—would you go and stay with her for a few days while I arrange things? Would you object to being married in the village church?'

'No. I'd like that very much, but perhaps your grandmother . . . I'm a stranger . . .'

'Not quite, you have met her—she brought her companion to see me.'

'Oh, so she knows who I am?' She sighed. 'That I'm the caretaker?'

He nodded. 'Oh, yes. She also knows that you're a very nice girl who will make me a good wife.'

'I shall do my best.'

He leaned forward and took her hands in his. 'We are agreed that there will be no false sentiment between us? Friends, companions, willing to allow each other to enjoy privacy without rancour, enjoying each other's company, spending our leisure together if we so wish.'

'If that is what you want,' she said steadily. 'You will help me, won't you? You have friends—perhaps you entertain sometimes?'

'Fairly frequently.' He smiled suddenly. 'And now I shall be able to enjoy that . . .'

'No more marriage-minded ladies to vex you!' She gave a chortle of laughter. 'They will think that you have gone mad when they see me.'

'In that case they will no longer be our friends. Tell me, Arabella, have you enough money? You will want to buy some clothes perhaps?'

'I've enough to start with. I expect I shall want more clothes after we're married if I'm to look like a consultant's wife. You want me to go and stay with your grandmother—but I must do some shopping.'

'Of course you must. Let me see. If I can get the new caretaker to take over on Saturday instead of Sunday would a couple of hours on Saturday morning be enough? I'll drive you down in the afternoon. When you're there you could get to Bath—Butter could drive you there.'

'Who is Butter?' It was like turning the leaves of a book, discovering something fresh on every page.

'Oh, he and Mrs Butter run the house.'

'Then if you don't mind I'd rather shop there and spend Saturday morning packing up here. What about Percy and Bassett?'

'They will go with you, of course. You have some things you would like to keep from here?' His cool eyes swept the room. 'The china and silver and so on? I'll have the tea-chest delivered and it can be taken round to Little Venice. The furniture?'

'There's nothing I want to keep, only Mother's work table.' A dainty mahogany stand with a faded silk bag. 'When—when do you think we should marry?'

'A week—ten days' time? But only if you agree to that... If you have no objection we might marry on a Saturday morning and come back here on the Sunday.'

'So that you can see your patients on Monday? That seems a sensible idea.' She saw the look of relief on his face and reminded herself that their marriage was to be a friendly arrangement which mustn't interfere with his work.

He went presently. At the door he said, 'I very much dislike leaving you here, Arabella. Must you dust and clean?'

'Well, yes, it's my job, which I must do while I'm here ...'

He threw an arm round her shoulders. 'When we are married you need never touch a duster or a dish-mop for the rest of your days.'

'A prospect no girl could resist. Will you let me know when the new caretaker is coming so that I can be ready for him?'

'Tomorrow. Take care, my dear.'

She bustled through her chores—there were only two days to Saturday and there were things to be done. Her clothes would pass muster until she could go shopping; they weren't in the forefront of fashion but Titus wouldn't need to feel ashamed of her. There were her precious bits and pieces to pack carefully and the place to set to rights so that the new caretaker would get a good impression. She told the animals about it while she got their suppers and then she started to wrap up her china and silver with the exception of necessities for the next day or two. She went to bed much later than usual, happily planning what was still to be done.

Dr Marshall sent for her the next morning. 'Well, well,' he said jovially, 'so you are to leave us, although I hope that we shall see a great deal more of you in the future. Of course I never thought that you would be with us for long, Arabella, and may I say that I am truly delighted for you and Titus. I'm sure you will be very happy together. Titus has arranged for the new man to call this morning so that you can show him round and explain things. You can let Titus know when it is convenient for you to be fetched on Saturday. You must come to dinner and meet my wife, although I'm hoping you will ask me to give you away at your wedding in which case perhaps she might accompany me?'

'Of course,' said Arabella warmly. 'And thank you for saying you'll give me away. I—I haven't any family living nearby and in any case I don't think they would be interested.'

The new caretaker was a middle-aged man, a cheerful cockney who had been made redundant from the buses and was delighted to have a job and a home again. He was a widower, living in a room near the Elephant and Castle and only too happy to move away from there.

He inspected the basement and pronounced it first-rate. 'I'll 'ave ter get some bits and pieces of furniture,' he told her. 'I suppose you wouldn't leave the curtains and the matting? I'll pay yer, of course.'

'You can have them for nothing,' said Arabella, liking the man, 'and I'd be glad to leave the furniture and the saucepans and so on. You see, I'm going to marry and don't need any of them.'

'Cor, bless my soul—yer really mean it?'

'Yes, of course I do. I'm going to make us a cup of coffee and explain the job to you and presently, when the last morning patient has gone, I'll take you round and show you everything.'

'That's a nice little dog you've got there—and a cat. I've got a cat meself. No objection to 'aving 'er 'ere, I suppose?'

'Well, I was allowed to have Percy. Bassett isn't really allowed, only I found him and he hadn't anywhere to go. A cat's company though, isn't it?'

'That she is.' He looked around him. 'This is a bit of all right, I can tell you.'

'It's a good job and everyone's very kind. If you've finished your coffee we'll go upstairs. Could you come on Saturday morning about eleven o'clock? I'll leave the bed made up with clean sheets and there'll be milk and bread and some food in the pantry. After you've cleaned up you are free on Saturday. I went shopping then—there are all the shops you'll need five minutes' walk away. The narrow road on the left as you leave the house. The doctors like the doors to be shut and locked and bolted when they are not here and I check each evening before I go to bed. I expect Dr Marshall told you about answering the door? You'll find the receptionist, Miss Baird, very kind and helpful.'

He went away presently and she gobbled a sandwich and had more coffee before going upstairs to answer the door to the afternoon patients.

There had been no sign of Dr Tavener. It was Miss Baird who told her that he had gone to Birmingham and would not be back until Friday.

'I haven't had the chance to congratulate you, Arabella,' she said kindly, 'and wish you happy. Dr Tavener is a splendid man. I'm sure you will deal excellently with each other.'

Arabella thanked her. 'I don't quite know when we are to be married.'

'We shall miss you—all of us...'

'Thank you. I have been very happy here, you know. The new caretaker seems to be a very nice man, and so delighted to have work again.'

She was up very early on the Saturday morning, dusting and Hoovering and putting fresh flowers in their vases, and after a quick breakfast she changed into her suit, tied her overall over it and checked that everything was ready for Mr Flinn, before going upstairs ready to open the door.

He came punctually and since there was a lull in the stream of patients she took him downstairs to show him the pantry, explain about the milkman, and point out the list of usual directions she had left on the table.

Dr Tavener hadn't been in and despite her good sense she felt a prickle of apprehension that he had forgotten all about her or, even worse, had second thoughts about marrying her. The idea was absurd, she admitted to herself, and it was only because she was excited and uncertain—a fact borne out by his quiet arrival just before noon.

His hello was friendly and the placid enquiry as to whether she was ready ruffled her feelings. Anyone would think, she reflected crossly, that getting married was a fairly regular event in his life.

He was in no hurry to go either, but stood talking to Mr Flinn before remarking that he would send Butter round for the tea-chest some time that afternoon, scooping Bassett up under one arm and picking up Percy's basket with the other hand. 'Said goodbye to everyone?' he wanted to know.

'Yes,' said Arabella and shook Mr Flinn's hand and wished him well. In the car she said, 'I thought you said that Butter lived in your other house?'

'Quite right, he does. He's coming up today so that he can drive you down this evening. I've an appointment I must keep this afternoon but I'll come down later tonight. My grandmother is expecting you and Butter will take good care of you.'

If I were beautiful and charming and well-dressed, thought Arabella crossly, I would throw a tantrum, make a scene and have him grovelling for treating me like a parcel.

She went red when he said, 'I'm sorry I can't drive you down—this is something which cropped up this morning and it really must be dealt with.'

He glanced at her pink cheeks and smiled a little. 'Would you agree to the wedding next Saturday? Will that give you enough time to do your shopping?'

'Yes, thank you. Are Percy and Bassett to come with me to your other house?'

'Of course, and we'll bring them back with us on the Sunday. Bassett is turning into a very well-mannered dog and Percy is happy wherever you are, isn't he?'

'Yes. You don't think they'll run away?'

'At the manor? No. There's a high brick wall around the grounds and Beauty's brother, Duke, will keep an eye on them.'

Mrs Turner met them at the door and Arabella, who had been secretly nervous of her reception, was relieved at the warmth of her welcome.

'I've been telling the doctor he should take a wife these years past,' said Mrs Turner, leading her away to tidy herself. 'And with respect, Miss Lorimer, I think he's chosen well. I'll be glad to serve you.'

'Why, thank you, Mrs Turner.' Arabella stopped and held out a hand. 'Shall we shake on that? I'm sure you know exactly how the doctor likes things done.'

'Indeed I do. Easygoing he may be, but he likes things just so, as you might say. When will you be marrying, Miss Lorimer?'

'Next Saturday. I hope you'll come to the wedding; it's to be very quiet.'

'Nothing would keep me away, miss.'

Arabella was left to pat her already neat head to even more tidiness and add a little lipstick, and since she was feeling a little nervous she didn't hurry over it. Presently she went back into the hall and was instantly hailed by the doctor from a door at the end of it.

'In here, Arabella. We'll have a drink before lunch.' He held the door open for her as she went into the room. It was small and cosy with a bright fire and easy-chairs and rows of bookshelves. The window overlooked the garden and the canal and there was a round table under it with two mahogany dining chairs on either side of it.

'I have my breakfast here and you must use this room as your sitting-room—your mother's work table will look exactly right here, won't it?'

He pulled up a chair for her to one side of the fireplace and nodded to the three animals sitting in a tidy row before the fire—Bassett in the middle. 'I dare say Beauty will adopt him if Percy allows her to.'

He handed her a glass. 'Champagne—for we have something to celebrate, do we not, Arabella? Here's to us and our happy future together.'

Arabella drank. 'Oh, I do hope so,' she said fervently.

CHAPTER FIVE

IT WAS mid-afternoon when Arabella left with Butter in the dark blue Jaguar car which he had driven up. He had greeted her with obvious pleasure and gone away to the kitchen to have a quick lunch before taking her back and now she sat beside him, with the animals on the back seat, conscious that she should be feeling happy and content and aware of a faint prickle of unease. Titus had been kind and thoughtful of her comfort, putting her at ease in what might have been an awkward situation, but all the same she had sensed that he was relieved to see her go. Whatever it was— or whoever it was—he had to deal with that afternoon must have been important. A girlfriend? she wondered uneasily. After all, he had told her that he had fallen in and out of love many times. Perhaps whoever it was was unable to marry him? Married already, or just not wanting to be his wife. He would be going to say goodbye... She brooded over this sad fact of her imagination until it seemed to be true and, being a romantic girl at heart, she could have wept for him. Indeed, if she had been by herself she would have done so but Butter, after a lengthy silence, took it upon himself to tell her about the house they were going to.

'The house in Little Venice is nice enough,' he conceded, 'but the manor's a real home, as you might say. Not all that big but plenty of ground around it and a garden to be proud of, miss. Me and Mrs Butter, we've lived there for years. Served the doctor's father, we did. Very well-liked in the village he is, too. Old Mrs Tavener lives there too—got a companion and has rooms to herself. Under one roof, as it were, but independent, like.' He overtook a huge transporter and kept on in the fast lane.

He was a good driver; she had been surprised at that. He looked to be a very ordinary middle-aged man who would drive a family car at a steady forty miles an hour, and here he was whizzing along at almost twice that speed.

'Not going too fast for you, miss?'

'No, no, I like speed.'

'Now the doctor—he's one for speeding in that Rolls of his. Do you drive, miss?'

'I used to. A Rover.'

'Nice little car. There's a Mini in the garage at the manor, just right for getting around on your own.'

She supposed that she would be on her own for a good deal of her days. She tried to visualise her future and couldn't.

They were almost there and she longed for a cup of tea and at the same time wished that they could drive on for a long while yet because she was nervous of meeting Titus's grandmother. That they had already met wasn't any help for then she had been the caretaker, answering the door and hanging up coats and taking umbrellas. The old lady might hate the idea of her grandson marrying a working girl, never mind what he had said.

The village came in sight, small and red-roofed and stone-built, tucked away in a narrow valley between the hills, the church—much too big for its size—

standing in the centre, the one road running past it, uphill a little and turning sharply at the top.

She caught her first glimpse of the manor then, and sighed with delight. It made a lovely picture in the winter twilight, its windows lighted, and as Butter came to a stop before the door it was thrown open and a small, stout woman, oblivious of the cold, stood on the steps.

Arabella, helped from the car by Butter, clasped Bassett to her and crossed the sweep with him, carrying a muttering Percy in his basket.

'There now.' The little woman took Arabella's free hand and shook it. 'I'm Mrs Butter, miss, and very happy to welcome you. Come on in out of the cold— you'll be wanting a cup of tea, I'll be bound. Mrs Tavener and Miss Welling have had theirs this hour past but I'm to see that you have a cup before you do anything else, so let me have your coat and I'll fetch the tea tray. Butter, take the little dog and the cat into the garden and then they can be with Miss Lorimer before they have their suppers.'

'There's a lead tied on to Bassett's basket,' said Arabella, 'and Percy's harness. Shall I do it?'

'Leave it to me, miss,' said Butter comfortably. 'Just you go and have that tea and then Mrs Butter'll take you to Mrs Tavener's rooms.'

So Arabella found herself in no time at all in a small panelled room, softly lighted by wall sconces and table lamps, furnished in great comfort with easy-chairs and with a brisk fire burning in the old-fashioned grate.

'The master uses this room a great deal,' Mrs Butter told her as she arranged the tea tray on one of the tables. 'Comes in from walking the dogs, he does, "Mrs Butter," he says, "I'm famished." And he sits

down in his chair and he and the dogs between them
eat enough for a giant. Well, I mean to say he is a
giant, isn't he, miss? And a good man, never better!'

She paused on her way out. 'We're that pleased that
he's getting married. This house needs a mistress and
a pack of children.'

Arabella, slightly overwhelmed, smiled and nodded
and murmured and, left alone, drank her tea and then
ate the scones and jam. She was beginning to worry
about Bassett and Percy when the door opened and
Butter came in with Bassett prancing at his heels and
Percy under his arm. A black Labrador came in too,
nudging Bassett gently and going to Arabella to stare
at her with a mild eye. She scratched his head and he
sighed heavily with pleasure and then sat down before
the fire, and presently the puppy settled beside him.
Then, much to Arabella's surprise, Percy, after a few
tentative advances, sat down too.

'Now, if you are ready, miss,' said Butter, 'I'll take
you along to see Mrs Tavener. We can close the door
and leave these three to make friends.'

He noticed her hesitation. 'Never fear, miss, Duke's
as mild as milk and he loves cats too.'

The house, she discovered, was larger than she had
thought, with a great many passages and steps and
unexpected staircases. Mrs Tavener's apartments were
on the first floor, at the end of a passage at the back
of the house. Butter knocked on a door at its end and
Miss Welling answered it, greeting Arabella with a
smile and invited her in. 'Mrs Tavener is so looking
forward to seeing you again, Miss Lorimer. May I
wish you every happiness? We are all so delighted that
the doctor is to marry.'

She led the way along a small passage with several doors and opened the end one. The room beyond was large with a bay window at one end and rather over-full of furniture. It was also very warm for there was a great fire burning in the elegant fireplace. Mrs Tavener was sitting upright in a tall-backed chair, a book on her lap.

'Ah, Titus's bride. My dear, I am so happy to welcome you to our family—come here and kiss me.'

Arabella weaved her way carefully through the tables, chairs and display cabinets and kissed the elderly cheek and, bidden to sit down, sat.

'Titus telephoned not half an hour ago. Wanted to know if you had arrived. He was on the point of leaving—such a nuisance that he couldn't drive you down himself. But I believe this was a matter which he wished to deal with personally. It will be delightful to have you here for a few days, my dear. You must treat this house as your home, for that is what it will be. I live here with Miss Welling, but I promise you that I don't interfere or intrude into Titus's life—nor will I with you.' She smiled. 'I hope that if you want advice or just someone to talk to you won't hesitate to come and see me.'

Arabella liked the old lady. 'I expect I shall need a great deal of advice. You see, I know very little about Titus's private life.'

Mrs Tavener gave her a thoughtful look. 'Well, dear, I'm sure that he will tell you anything you want to know. I don't suppose you have had much opportunity to talk together.'

Which was true enough, reflected Arabella.

Presently Mrs Butter came to fetch her. 'I'll show you your room, miss, for the doctor will be here within

the hour and you'll want to be ready for him. I've
taken the liberty of unpacking your things.'

Her room was charming, furnished with yew and
applewood, its curtains pastel chintz, echoing the pale
colours of the carpet and the bedcover. She bathed,
resisting the wish to lie for ages in the warm water
and allow her thoughts to wander, and then, wearing
her only dress—needlecord in teal-blue, several years
out of date but still elegant—her face nicely made-up
and her hair neatly coiled, she went downstairs to the
small room again to find the animals still sitting, apparently on the best of terms and very content. The
carriage clock on the mantelpiece chimed the hour—
seven o'clock, she saw with something of shock—and
she wondered how much longer Titus would be.

He came in a few minutes later, Beauty with him.
'I'm sorry I wasn't here when you came down,' he
said cheerfully. 'I got here half an hour ago and I've
been in my study. You're quite comfortable? You've
seen Grandmother? Good. Butter and Mrs Butter are
looking after you, I hope?'

He sat down opposite her and Beauty edged her
way past him to sit beside Percy.

'They seem to have settled down very well—I hope
you will do the same, Arabella.'

She took care to sound pleasantly satisfied as well
as friendly. 'Oh, I'm sure I shall. This is a very
beautiful house, isn't it?'

'Yes. Tomorrow I'll take you over it and show you
the grounds. Will you come to church with me in the
morning?'

'Yes, I'd like that. Did you have a good
drive down?'

'Excellent. We must try and come here as often as possible and it would be very pleasant for me if you will come with me when I have to keep appointments out of town. I must go over to Leiden at the end of the month—just for a couple of days. I have friends there whom I think you will like.'

'They're Dutch?'

'He is—his wife is English. We'll come here for Christmas, of course.'

Her head on the pillow and half asleep, several hours later Arabella decided that even if she had had doubts she had them no longer. Being with Titus was like being with an old friend. He had been quite right—without deep feelings for each other they were able to behave towards each other like old and tried companions.

She woke in the night and just for one moment thought that she was in her basement room. She sat up in bed, worried because she couldn't feel the animals on her feet, and then remembered that they had settled to sleep quite happily with Titus's two dogs in the kitchen and that she was in a quite different room.

The rector came back with them after church the next morning and his wife came too, frankly curious about Arabella and full of questions about the wedding. Over sherry Titus parried her artfully put questions and when they had gone told Arabella that she was a splendid rector's wife but eager to know everyone's business. 'She'll be at the wedding, of course. You won't find ten o'clock in the morning too early? We will have lunch here with Grandmother afterwards and drive up to town in the afternoon.'

He crossed the room and took her arm. 'Come and look round the house before lunch.'

It was a roomy old place. Besides the vast drawing-room there was a dining-room, his study, the little room the animals seemed to consider was theirs, and a room overlooking the garden at the back and opening on to a conservatory. They stood at its open door for a few moments, surveying the wintry gardens. 'There's a swimming-pool at the end behind those rhododendrons and the kitchen garden is through that small doorway at the end of the wall.' He turned away. 'Come upstairs—we'll leave the kitchen for the moment or we shall get under Mrs Butter's feet.'

At the top of the staircase he crossed the circular landing and opened double doors. 'This will be your room.'

It was large, with windows opening on to a small balcony, and carpeted in the colour of clotted cream. The curtains were rose-patterned and silk, as was the bedspread. The bed was a four-poster with a cream canopy highlighting the sheen of its mahogany. There was a vast dressing-table in the same wood, bedside tables bearing pink-shaded lamps and a chaise longue and small comfortable chairs in misty blue. It would be an enchanting place in which to wake up each morning. 'Oh, it's beautiful,' said Arabella, rotating slowly. 'What's through those doors?'

'Bathroom and beyond that a dressing-room. The other door is a clothes closet.'

Beyond the bathroom and dressing-room there was another bedroom, smaller and rather austere. 'My room,' said Titus briefly, and led her through another door back to the landing.

She lost count of the bedrooms she was shown and followed him up a smaller staircase to the floor above. The rooms here were smaller but well-furnished and at one end of the passage there was a baize door

'The Butters have a flat,' he explained. 'There are two housemaids but they come each day.'

He glanced at his watch. 'We had better go down to lunch. This afternoon if you would like to we will go round the grounds.'

On their way downstairs he stopped. 'I entirely forgot,' he told her gravely, and took a small box from his pocket. 'Your ring...'

She took it slowly and opened its velvet lid. The ring was a half-hoop of splendid diamonds in an old-fashioned setting. 'It's been in the family for a long time—gets handed down from one bride to the next. I hope it fits.'

He made no move to put it on her finger. Arabella told herself that would have been sentimental nonsense anyway. It fitted well and she held up her hand to admire it. 'It's very beautiful.'

However unsentimental the giving had been, she mustn't sound ungrateful. She added warmly, 'Thank you very much, Titus. I shall wear it with pride.'

She smiled up at him and surprised a look on his face which puzzled her, but even as she looked it had gone and been replaced with his habitual bland expression. She must have fancied it.

At lunch old Mrs Tavener said, 'Ah—you're wearing the ring. You have pretty hands, Arabella. What do you think of your future home?'

They talked about the house and its history, the village and the people who lived there, and when the meal was finished the old lady went away to her room.

'Miss Welling goes down to the rectory for lunch on Sundays,' she explained, 'and Mrs Butter settles me for a nap. I dare say I shall see you at tea.'

After she had gone they sat for a little while over their coffee in the drawing-room, the animals stretched out before the fire, until Titus said, 'Fetch a coat and I'll take you round the gardens before the light goes.'

Even in the wintry weather the gardens were a great delight, and when he opened the door into the kitchen garden she said delightedly, 'Oh, it is—it reminds me . . .' and fell silent.

'Of your garden at home? I suppose that most of the country houses in these parts have these walled gardens. Come and see the greenhouses. I inherited the gardener with the house; he's old and crotchety and grows everything under the sun. I took on his grandson this summer—he will be just as good in time.'

'Only an old man and a boy for all this?' She waved an arm around her at the orderly rows, the bare fruit trees and the fruit bushes.

'A couple of men come in several times a week to give a hand with the heavy work. Come this way.'

She stayed where she was. 'Titus, I'm not sure . . . that is, I'm not sure if I can live up to you and all this.'

He took her arm and began to walk along the path bordering the rows of cabbages and leeks. 'Ah, now you can understand why I need a wife—someone to help me live up to it as well.'

'But it's your home.'

'And will be yours too . . .'

'You have an answer for everything.'

'No, no. The last thing I wish to do is coerce you. You have only to say, my dear, and you will be as free as air again.'

That brought her up short once more. 'You really want me to marry you?' she asked. 'You're quite sure?'

'Quite sure.' He bent and kissed her cheek and took her arm again. 'Come with me, I've something to show you.'

He flung an arm around her shoulders and her doubts melted away. Surely being his wife wouldn't be as difficult as caretaking. 'Not another garden?' she asked as he went through a second arched doorway. 'Oh, stables.' She peered around her in the afternoon gloom. 'Do you ride?'

'Yes, as often as possible.' He opened the first stable door and said, 'Come inside.'

There was a pony there, and there was a small donkey too, and both raised their heads as she went in. The pony whinnied and came to meet her, followed by the donkey.

'Why,' said Arabella, 'it's Bess—and Jerry too!' She went between them, hugging them, murmuring into their ears and stroking them.

'A wedding present,' said Titus quietly. 'Here—sugar for Bess and a carrot for Jerry.'

She ignored that. 'Titus, oh, Titus, how can I ever thank you? It's the most marvellous thing to happen to me since I left home.' She didn't see the lift of his eyebrows and his faint smile. She left the animals and stretched up to kiss his cheek. 'You have no idea . . .' she began, and burst into tears.

He put an arm around her and let her weep into his shoulder. Presently she gave a great sniff and mut-

tered in a sodden voice, 'Oh, I'm so sorry, what a
way to behave. Only, I'm so happy.'

He offered a large snowy handkerchief. 'It's nice
to meet old friends again,' he observed in a
comfortable voice. 'They're in good shape—you don't
ride Bess any more, I imagine?'

'No, not since I was about fifteen. She's very old—
so is Jerry.'

'Yes, I suppose so. Well, they can enjoy the rest of
their lives here. There's a paddock beyond the yard
here—we've had them out for a few hours each day.
Old Spooner's grandson—Dicky—is splendid with
animals. You can safely leave them in his care.'

She gave him a wide watery smile. 'I can't keep
saying thank you,' she began.

'No need. I am delighted to have pleased you. Shall
we go back to the house? I have to go directly after
tea.'

She gave the animals a final hug, assured them that
she would see them the following day, and walked
back to the house, happily unaware that her unre-
markable face wasn't improved by tearstains and a
very pink nose.

Back at the house she went to her room and was
horrified at the sight of her face in the looking-glass.
At least it had been almost dark outside; Titus would
have noticed nothing. She repaired the damage,
smoothed her hair and went down for tea—a meal
taken in Mrs Tavener's company with Miss Welling
sitting like a shadow beside her. She still looked
apologetic but Arabella noticed that she ate a hearty
tea. She thought that probably Miss Welling was perfectly happy despite her downtrodden expression—
she was certainly treated as an old friend by the

Taveners and she had beamed her delight when she
had wished Arabella happy. It was a pleasant meal
but soon Titus got to his feet. 'I must go,
Grandmother. I'll be down next Saturday morning,
early. I'll see Butter about that.'

He stooped to kiss the old lady's cheek, shook Miss
Welling's hand and whistled to Beauty. From the look
he gave her, Arabella guessed quite rightly that she
was to see him out of the house. She followed him
into the hall where Butter was waiting.

Dr Tavener's directions took only a minute or so
before Butter tactfully withdrew, leaving Arabella and
Titus facing each other at the door. If she had hoped
for anything of even a slightly romantic nature, she
wasn't going to get it.

'Take Duke for a run each day, will you? Butter
usually takes him but I dare say you'll go at a pace
to suit Duke better. Let Butter know what day you
want to go shopping. Don't bother to buy too much;
you can shop all you want to when we get back to
London. Take care of that puppy of yours and
Percy—they seem to have settled down very nicely.'

He didn't ask if *she* had settled down nicely. A
flicker of resentment flamed inside her and died when
she remembered Bess and Jerry.

'Drive carefully,' she said, and bent to pat Beauty's
head.

He said, surprising her, 'You are happy, Arabella?'

'Thank you, yes, I am, Titus.'

He opened the door, kissed her briefly on a cheek,
ushered Beauty into the car, got in himself and drove
away with a casual wave as he went.

'After all, what did I expect?' Arabella asked
herself, and went back to discuss a wedding outfit with
Mrs Tavener.

Everyone was very kind; she was surrounded by
warmth and comfort and people anxious that she
should feel at home and happy. Although she had her
meals with Mrs Tavener and Miss Welling she had the
rest of the days to herself and despite the wintry
weather she took Duke for long walks, getting to know
the surrounding countryside. She had coffee with the
rector and his wife too. The rector's wife was a dear
little woman who took it for granted that Arabella
and Titus were deeply in love. 'So very nice to have
you at the manor,' she confided to Arabella. 'Titus
has been single for too long. I look forward to you
living there—it's a lovely old place, isn't it? Marvellous for children too.'

She misinterpreted Arabella's pink cheeks and
smiled cosily.

Halfway through the week Butter drove Arabella
to Bath, arranged to pick her up again in the late
afternoon and drove off, leaving her to the exciting
business of buying clothes. Every penny she pos-
sessed was in her purse—not a great deal of money
but enough for what she intended to buy.

It was lunchtime before she had found what she
wanted: a jacket and skirt in a fine wool in the blue
of a winter sky. There was a matching silk top to go
with them and, after a bit of poking around, she found
a velvet hat with a high crown and a tiny brim. Pulled
well down over her eyes, she fancied, it improved
her looks...

It had been an expensive outfit so she went in search of the high street stores and found a pleated checked skirt with a three-quarter-length jacket to go with it, a couple of sweaters, some undies and a simple dress in stone-coloured cotton jersey—and she was almost penniless. She had pretty shoes and several pairs of good gloves salvaged from earlier days. She would have liked a handbag but that must wait. She ate a very overdue lunch in a small and cheap café and walked to where Butter was to pick her up.

Back in her room at the manor, she spread her purchases out on the bed. They were all right as far as they went but she would need to go shopping once she was married. Her wardrobe was woefully inadequate for the wife of an eminent physician. She tried on the hat and decided that it had been worth every penny of its price.

At dinner that evening she assured Mrs Tavener that she had had a most successful day shopping. 'I won't tell you what I've bought—I'd like it to be a surprise.'

Titus had telephoned once during the week. He would drive down with his best man—a friend of long-standing—and arrive for breakfast. Dr Marshall and his wife would arrive on the Friday evening—Butter had his instructions; they would stay the night at the manor. He would see her on Saturday morning at the church.

He had rung off with the kind of goodbye she might have expected from an older brother.

Mrs Butter, a great one for tradition, brought her breakfast up to her room on Saturday morning. 'The doctor's here, miss,' she said breathlessly. 'Dr and Mrs Marshall are having breakfast with him now. Do eat up—I'll be back in half an hour or so to run your bath. You mustn't be late at the church.'

Arabella ate her breakfast, for she had the good sense to know that she would be too excited to eat anything else for the rest of the day. She dressed carefully, wishing to make the best of herself; it was after all her wedding-day. She didn't look too bad, she considered, inspecting herself in the pier glass. It would have been nice if she had been pretty but since Titus wasn't in love with her she supposed that that didn't matter very much, and the right clothes, the right make-up and a visit to a good hairdresser would certainly improve her looks.

It was time to go. Mrs Butter came to fetch her, wearing an overpowering hat and a buttonhole in her winter coat.

'You look lovely,' she said. 'Just like a bride should. The master's gone to the church and Dr Marshall's waiting for you.'

Dr Marshall kissed her. 'You look beautiful—that's a pretty thing you're wearing and I do like the hat. Let's go.'

It was to have been a very quiet wedding but half the village had crammed into the church. Arabella hesitated at the door but Dr Marshall nipped her arm. 'Titus wants you to have these,' he whispered, and handed her a little bouquet of roses and miniature lilies, pale pink, and mixed in with them were lily-of-the-valley, miniature daffodils and small sprigs of rosemary. She buried her nose in its fragrance and then took Dr Marshall's arm and walked serenely down the aisle, her eyes on Titus's broad back. When they were almost by him he turned to look at her and smile and she smiled back. Two old friends meeting, she thought in a muddled way. Everything was going to be all right.

She made her vows in a small firm voice, meaning to keep every word of them. The future was unpredictable but she intended to do her best to be the kind of wife he wanted. She didn't hear a word of the rector's short homily, so busy was she with her own thoughts.

The rest of the day passed in a dream; she smiled and talked and shook hands and was kissed, drank a little too much champagne, cut the cake with Titus's firm hand upon hers and at length found herself in the Rolls with the animals crowded in the back and all of them covered in confetti.

Once they were clear of the village Titus pulled into a lay-by.

'We should have brought a dustpan and brush with us,' he observed. 'Come here and be brushed down.'

They laughed about it together while she did the same for him and then the more difficult task of getting the confetti out of whiskery faces and furry coats commenced.

'That's better,' said Titus. 'Now I can see you. I like the hat!'

'Thank you, and thank you too for the beautiful flowers. It was a very successful wedding, wasn't it?'

'Indeed, yes. Now we will embark upon a successful marriage. Quite a different thing but one to which I look forward.'

'Me too,' said Arabella.

Mrs Turner had been at the wedding and Butter had left with her an hour or so before they had. She would be at Little Venice by the time they got there, ready to welcome them, and Butter would have started the drive back to the manor, anxious not to miss the party to be held in the village pub to celebrate the wedding.

Dr Tavener made good speed; there was very little traffic and although dusk was falling the road was clear but it was almost dark when he drew up before his house. All the lights were on and Mrs Turner flung open the door with a flourish.

'That's the best wedding I've ever been to,' she assured them as they went indoors. 'All the lovely flowers and the organ, and you, madam, looked a fair treat.'

Titus went to let the animals out and she said, 'Tea's all ready in the drawing-room. I'll see to the animals—you must both be needing a cup.'

'You're a jewel, Mrs Turner. Will you take Mrs Tavener up to her room first? I'll take the dogs and Percy into the garden—perhaps you would feed them presently?'

Arabella followed Mrs Turner up the staircase to a room at the back of the house, overlooking the canal. It was very large with doors opening on to a wrought-iron balcony and furnished in much the same style as her room at the manor—soft pastel colours, a wide four-poster bed and a dressing-table of applewood. There were a couple of comfortable chairs and pretty lamps on the tables, and delicate water-colours on the cream satin-striped walls.

'The bathroom's through that door and the dressing-room's on the other side, madam, and you've only to ask for anything you would like.'

'Mrs Turner, I'm sure everything is just perfect. I hope you will give me your advice . . .'

'That I will, with pleasure. Not lived in London
before you went to the doctor's rooms?'

'No, my home was in the country, near Sherborne.
Not anywhere as large as the manor but a nice ram-
bling sort of house. This house is beautiful, though.
It isn't like living in London at all and it's so quiet.'
She turned from the window. 'You do have help in
the house, Mrs Turner?'

'That I do. Maisie comes in each morning—a good
girl, does her work as it should be done and always
cheerful. I'll be going down to make the tea, madam,
you must be fair parched.'

Later, sitting opposite Titus in the drawing-room,
talking in a desultory manner while he went through
his letters, Arabella had the strange feeling that they
had been married for years, sitting in each other's
company like an elderly married couple, easy with
each other, comfortably silent if they wished. It was
reassuring and what she supposed she had expected,
only there was a vague doubt at the back of her head
that Titus might discover one day that there was still
a lot of life left before they reached the cosy stage.
Supposing he met someone—some beautiful woman—
and fell in love? He wouldn't be content to sit by the
fire then, would he? She wasn't sure but she thought
that he had never really looked at her, only as one
would look at some familiar friend or a member of
the family. He was comfortable with her, she was sure
of that, and he liked her, but wouldn't he find that
insufficient after a time? Would he miss his dinner
parties and the divorced ladies bent on amusing him?

She frowned a little; she mustn't start thinking such
thoughts on her wedding-day. She would make plans

to improve her looks, buy clothes, meet people, give smart little dinner parties ...

Dr Tavener, watching her, wondered what she was thinking. He said, 'It's been a long day. I dare say you are tired?'

'Well, yes, I am.' She uttered the fib with composure. 'You won't mind if I go up to bed?'

The alacrity with which he went to open the door was hardly flattering. She wasn't sure what she had expected; it certainly wasn't his pleasant goodnight. 'Sleep well, Will breakfast at eight-thirty suit you?'

'Yes, thank you. Do we go to church in the morning?'

'If you would come with me I should be very glad.'

'Well, of course I will. Goodnight, Titus.'

He kissed her cheek. 'No regrets?'

'Not a single one. I'd like to go to the kitchen and say goodnight to Percy and Bassett.'

'Of course. Have them in your room if you would like that.'

'No, no. I'm sure they are happy with Beauty.'

She slipped past him on her way to the kitchen and she didn't look back.

CHAPTER SIX

ARABELLA wasn't in the least tired. Curled up in the vast bed, she reviewed the day. It had gone without a hitch but then she had known it would; Titus wouldn't have stood for less than perfection. She had enjoyed the wedding and she felt at home here in this comfortable house by the canal although the manor house had her heart—besides, Bessy and Jerry were there. They would go there very often, Titus had said, and she knew him well enough to know that she could rely on him not to go back on his word. She wondered how she would fill her days, and went to sleep while she was still pondering that.

They breakfasted together, the two dogs and Percy lined up between them before the fire, discussing when they would go to the manor again, which day Arabella would like to go shopping, the best walks for the dogs—a pleasant, undemanding conversation. Arabella, notwithstanding her doubts of the previous night, felt very much at her ease.

'We'll take these two into the park this afternoon?' he suggested. 'Bassett needs a good run and Beauty will keep an eye on him.' He glanced at his watch. 'We can walk to church—it's only ten minutes or so. I've some telephoning—can we meet in an hour?'

She wandered round the house, getting to know her way around it, and then she went into the garden with the animals. It was a chilly morning and she was wearing her suit; her winter coat had seen better days and she hesitated to wear it to church. Probably Titus was known there and people might think her a very shabby sort of wife. It was fortunate that she still had a felt hat which would go very well with the suit—a dateless hat, plain and elegant and made by a well-known hatter.

He was waiting for her when she went downstairs. She was conscious of his eyes raking her person and went pink. 'Very nice,' he told her, 'but shouldn't you be wearing a thicker coat?'

She said simply, 'My winter coat is too old—you'd be ashamed of me.'

'Never. But you will be happier without it. To-morrow you shall go to the shops and start to buy whatever you need, Arabella. I don't mean any shops—I've an account at Harrods; you'll go there, please, and buy anything and everything which may take your fancy.'

'That's a risky remark to make to a woman.'

'Not to you! As soon as I have time I'll get you settled with an allowance; in the meantime use Harrods.'

'It's a very expensive shop. I haven't been there for years.'

They were walking to church along the quiet streets. 'Well, now you can have a browse round and see if it still suits your taste. I'll give them a ring in the morning and let you have my account number.'

'Thank you, but you must let me know how much I can spend—I haven't the least idea.'

He mentioned a sum which brought her to a halt. 'You can't mean that—why, it's a small fortune!'

He took her arm and walked her along. 'My dear Arabella, you are now my wife and I am proud of you, therefore, like all husbands, I want you to have all the pretty things you would like. Besides, now that I am a safely married man we shall have to entertain and I warn you that before you know where you are you will find yourself sitting on committees, drinking coffee and organising bazaars. For all these occasions you will need clothes. You like clothes, presumably?'

'Like them? Of course I do. I shall run mad at Harrods—it will take more than one day's shopping, too.'

'Take as many days as you like. I've a busy week ahead of me. We will go down to the manor at the weekend, though, and the following week I have to go to Leiden and I would like you to go with me.'

'I'd like that very much. My passport's out of date, though.'

'We'll see about that in the morning.'

They had reached the church and sure enough a number of people there greeted Titus as they took their places in one of the pews. She enjoyed the service even if once or twice her thoughts strayed to the shopping delights ahead of her.

Mrs Turner was a splendid cook—the roast beef was done to a turn, the vegetables were just right and the queen of puddings which followed was deliciously light. They had their coffee and since the winter days were getting short took the dogs into the park, walking until it was dusk, and Bassett was so tired that Arabella tucked him under one arm while Beauty raced to and fro, apparently inexhaustible.

They had tea round the fire and spent a pleasant evening discussing the week ahead. He would take her out to dinner during the week, he told her, adding with a twinkle, 'So that you will have a chance to air one of your new dresses.'

She sparkled. 'Oh, how lovely. Where?'

'Claridge's—we can dance.' He watched the colour come into her cheeks. 'I should be home early on Wednesday—shall we go then?'

'Oh, yes, please.' For a moment she was lost in a pleasant dream—transformed into a beauty overnight, wearing a gorgeous dress, making the kind of conversation which would set him smiling. She could at least have a try. Suddenly she wanted him to notice her, not just as a friend and companion but as an attractive woman...

'What plan are you hatching in that neat head of yours?' he wanted to know. 'We'll go down to the manor at the weekend and lay our plans for the trip to Leiden.'

Presently they dined, well pleased with each other's company so that later, Arabella, getting ready for bed, reflected that living with Titus was going to be a success. Of course it was early days yet but they had made a good beginning. They might even, she thought wistfully, become fond of each other in time. She had no illusions about his falling in love with her—if he hadn't lost his heart to all the charming females he must have known he wasn't likely to lose it to her. She chuckled about that and then went to sleep on a sigh.

They breakfasted together quite early and Arabella, aware that Titus wished to sift through his post, checking the various reports on his patients, did no more than wish him a cheerful good morning. Later, she thought hopefully, she would have post of her own. She had plenty to think about. She had wakened early and made a list of the clothes she would buy; now she reviewed it mentally, adding a few articles she had overlooked, trying to guess what everything would cost. She gave a guilty start when Titus said suddenly, 'Remember, Arabella, if you go shopping today, buy what suits you and don't look at the price labels.'

'Don't you want to know how much I've spent?'

'No. I'll pay the bills when they arrive and if they're too wildly extravagant I shall tell you so.' He smiled across the table. 'I gave you some idea of how much you might spend but I shan't cavil at a few hundred more.'

He left the house presently and she took the dogs and Percy into the garden. Beauty had already had an early morning run with Titus and Bassett was happy enough running around, teasing the patient Beauty and chasing an indignant Percy. They all went back indoors presently and Arabella went to the kitchen to talk to Mrs Turner.

'Will you take me round the house one day?' she asked. 'And tell me what the doctor likes and doesn't like—and I'd love to do the shopping sometimes if you would tell me what to buy.'

'Lor' bless you, madam, it'll be a pleasure to take you round the cupboards and pantry. There's china and linen and silver you must inspect and the tradesmen's bills. If you would come each morning we could discuss the meals for the day and make a list of the shopping if it's needed.'

'I'm going out now, Mrs Turner; I expect I'll be gone for quite a while. Would you please look after Beauty, Bassett and Percy?' She couldn't resist saying, 'I'm going to buy clothes.'

Mrs Turner looked positively motherly. 'And what could be nicer?' she wanted to know and added, 'But mind and have lunch, madam—shopping's tiring.'

Arabella wore the suit and felt hat; they were hardly high fashion but her shoes and gloves would pass muster anywhere. Mindful of Titus's request that she should take a taxi, she did so, feeling extravagant but it was a nice build-up to her day. She went through Harrods' elegant doors and began the delightful task of spending money.

By mid-morning she had acquired a winter coat— tobacco-brown cashmere—a brown and cream knitted three-piece, a jersey dress in copper, a beech-brown wool skirt, a cashmere cardigan and several blouses. She had a cup of coffee then, got her second wind, and went to look at dresses.

The choice was endless but she had a very good idea of what she wanted. By lunchtime she had tried on and bought a deep rose-pink dress in crêpe de Chine with a tucked bodice and a gored skirt which floated round her as she walked, a silk velvet dress in forest-green—very simple with a narrow skirt, long tight sleeves and a square neckline and, since she couldn't resist them, a wide midnight-blue skirt and an evening blouse with long full sleeves and a ruffled neck.

She went to the restaurant and had an omelette and coffee and decided that she had bought enough for one day. She had kept a rough check of the prices and although everything had cost a good deal there was still plenty over. Undies, shoes and a suit, she decided, as she was being taken back to her new home in a taxi loaded down with dress-boxes. It had begun to rain and she prudently added a raincoat to her list.

She had lunched late and Mrs Turner offered her tea as soon as she had got indoors. 'Well, just a quick cup,' said Arabella, 'before I take everything upstairs.'

'I'll see they go to your room, madam. Just you sit down and have that tea. Shopping can be tiring.'

So Arabella had her tea and presently, with the animals trailing stealthily behind her, went to her room. Here they arranged themselves tidily in a corner and watched her while she undid her packages and inspected what she had bought. She couldn't resist trying some of them on; she was twirling round in the pink crêpe de Chine when there was a knock on the door. It would be Mrs Turner, come to remind her that it had gone six o'clock and the doctor would be home presently. Arabella turned a guilty face to the door. 'Mrs Turner—do come in...'

Only it was Titus. She stopped in mid-twirl. 'Titus— I forgot the time—I thought it was Mrs Turner, come to tell me to come downstairs. I'm sorry—I did mean to be there, waiting for you...'

'Sitting with your knitting and the drinks poured?' He laughed then. 'My dear girl, you in that pink dress do me much more good than a soberly occupied wife.'

He cast his eyes round the room, strewn with clothes and tissue paper. 'You've made a start,' he commented drily. 'Will you wear this on Wednesday?'

She felt shy. 'If you would like me to. There are other dresses—I've bought an awful lot.'

'Splendid. I wondered where Beauty had got to. One of an admiring audience, I see.'

'Do you mind? I mean that they came upstairs with me? They were glad to see me.'

He crossed the room and took her hand. 'I'm glad to see you too, Arabella.' He kissed her briefly. 'Come

down and have a drink before dinner. I'll take these
three into the garden for a few minutes.'

He went away, whistling to the animals, who
trooped after him, leaving her to get out of the pink
dress and into the jersey dress, do her hair and do
things to her face in a perfunctory way.

Dressed and ready on the Wednesday evening, she
took stock of her person in the pier glass. The pink
dress certainly gave an illusion of prettiness and between bouts of shopping on the previous day she had
found time to buy the very best of face creams and
powders and have her hair shampooed and cut.
Indeed, fired by enthusiasm, she had tried out various
new hairstyles but none of them seemed right. She
ended up pinning her mousy locks on top of her head
as she had done for years.

Perhaps it was the pink dress which made the
evening such a success, although hardly a romantic
one. Titus had had a busy day and she was a good
listener. A good deal of their dinner was taken up
with his comments and observations on treatments,
medicines and the art of the physician as opposed to
that of the surgeon. Arabella listened with interest,
filing away some of the longer words she had never
heard before so that she could look them up later and
know what he was talking about next time.

The waiter had come to offer them coffee when
Titus asked, 'Would you like to dance? It seems a pity
not to display that pretty dress.'

She got up at once, making some cheerful remark
about the band while under the pink bodice she
seethed with a sudden ill-temper. He might have made
some pleasant remark about her person, never mind
if it wasn't true. She was no beauty but she was aware

that she looked attractive against the luxurious surroundings. Never mind the lack of looks, she told
herself, you know how to dance ...

She certainly did. She was light on her feet, as pliant
as a reed and a graceful dancer. Titus, a good dancer
himself, after the first few moments bent his head to
say quietly in her ear, 'It's like dancing with a
moonbeam! What a treasure I have married—not only
a first-rate plumber but a delightful dancer. We must
do this more often before I get too middle-aged!'

She looked up at that. 'Middle-aged? Of course
you're not. Aren't you supposed to be in your prime?'

'Why, thank you, Arabella, you encourage me to
fend off the encroaching years.' He smiled down at
her. 'Do you know you're attracting a great many admiring glances?'

'Oh, no, I didn't.' She had gone pink. 'I expect its
the dress ...'

He stared down at the top of her neat head, smiling
a little. He found her company delightful; she was so
very natural, so unassuming, so ready to fall in with
his plans and wishes. She made no effort to attract
him either, and that, after the scheming young ladies
he had from time to time considered himself in love
with, was something that he was already appreciating.

They went down to the manor at the weekend and,
since it was cold clear weather, they walked for miles
with Beauty and Duke bounding ahead and Bassett
doing his small best to keep up with them. Arabella,
scooping him up, said, 'Perhaps we should have left
him with Percy—he's still so very small.'

'He has the heart of a lion. Let me have him; he
can sit inside my jacket.' He slowed his stride so that
she could keep up. 'We go to Holland on Thursday.

I think it might be a good idea if we brought this lot down before we go. Butter can look after them and Mrs Butter dotes on Percy. Are you looking forward to going?'

'Yes, I am. Will you be away all day?'

'Most of it, but I'm sure you'll get on with Cressida. I've known Aldrik since we were students. Leiden isn't a large place but there are some good shops and plenty to see. You will be invited to the dinner which marks the end of the seminar—black ties and long dresses.'

'But everyone will be Dutch ...'

'Well, I'm not, for a start. Besides, everyone there will speak English.'

'I think it might be fun.'

Titus, looking at her glowing face, found rather to his surprise that he agreed with her.

They had tea with Mrs Tavener before they went back to London. The old lady, with Miss Welling in close attendance, wanted a blow-by-blow account of their life there. 'It is a great deal more healthy here than in your London house,' she declared. 'Arabella's looks have improved a great deal since you arrived yesterday.' She broke off to take stock of Arabella, who blushed and looked into her teacup and thus missed Titus's long thoughtful stare. 'Of course,' went on the old lady, 'once the children come along, you will have to spend more time here; they'll thrive in the country air.'

Arabella went on looking into her teacup, while wishing it could give her a suitable answer. It was Titus who said easily, 'You are quite right, Grandmother, small children are happiest in the country. I hated leaving here when I was first sent to boarding-school.'

A successful red herring which led the old lady to reminisce until it was time for them to leave.

If he even mentions it, thought Arabella, sitting silently beside him in the car, I'll throw something at him.

He never mentioned it, but talked easily of this and that so that by the time they were back at Little Venice she had managed to forget about it. All the same, she wished that they could have said something about it, laughed over it together, made a joke of it. It was the first time, she reflected, that they had avoided talking about something and she felt awkward about it. It was a good thing that Titus appeared to have forgotten about it, but perhaps he hadn't felt anything other than an amused interest in his grandmother's remarks.

They left early in the morning on Thursday to take the dogs and Percy to the manor, had a quick lunch there and then, after Arabella had raced down to the stables to make sure that the pony and the donkey were safe and well, they drove to catch the night ferry from Harwich. It was a long journey but Arabella, snug in her winter coat, her feet encased in fashionable boots, enjoyed it. They sped smoothly along the motorway until they reached the turning and circled round London to Watford, and then on to Hatfield, where they stopped for a late tea. It was a small café cosily lit and chintzy with very ladylike waitresses in flowered aprons; the tea was hot and plentiful and the buttered crumpets were delicious. Arabella sank her splendid teeth into them with a contented sigh.

'This is fun,' she said.

Titus found himself agreeing with her, reflecting that when he was with her he felt ten years younger.

They drove on presently and went on board the ferry. After dinner Arabella went to her cabin and despite the rough crossing slept soundly. Titus, watching her enjoying an early breakfast of rolls and coffee, smiled to himself. Their marriage was going to be a success; she was not only a good companion, she was sensible—accepting situations without fuss, undemanding of his attention and time and, he had to admit, really quite pretty now that she had new clothes. He studied her from lowered lids as she buttered a roll. What was more, she was dressed exactly as he would like to see her...

Leiden was less than half an hour's drive away. Arabella got glimpses of it as Titus drove through the town and presently turned into a narrow street lined with gabled houses, old and beautifully maintained. He helped her out, took her arm and urged her across the narrow cobbled pavement and pulled the wrought-iron bellpull beside an elegant front door. It was opened by an elderly rather bony-faced woman and a very large St Bernard dog, accompanied by a small insignificant beast. The woman smiled and the doctor said, 'Mies, how nice to see you again.' He patted the dogs' heads and added, 'Arabella, this is Mies—Cressida's housekeeper.'

She shook hands and was ushered inside as a small young woman came racing down the staircase. 'Titus—I should have been on the doorstep!' She lifted her face for his kiss and turned to Arabella. 'I'm Cressida—I'm so glad to meet you, Arabella.' She beamed happily, her lovely eyes sparkling from a very ordinary face. 'Aldrik has had to go to the hospital but he'll be back before lunch. Come on in and have some coffee. Titus, do go into the drawing-room— I'm going to take Arabella upstairs.'

Arabella followed her hostess upstairs, relieved at finding her so friendly. She had been a little worried that Cressida could have been a statuesque blonde and talked down to her. Instead here was this nice girl the same size as herself and certainly no beauty, although she looked so happy that she could have passed as beautiful.

'Titus said he would be late back each evening— seminars and things,' Cressida said vaguely, 'so I've put you in here and there's a dressing-room next door so that he needn't disturb you if it's the small hours.' She sat down on the bed. 'This was my room—I mean when Aldrik brought me back here—just for a night, then he took me to Friesland to a friend's house to look after some children.' She smiled gently. 'He's nice—I do hope you'll like him. We think Titus is a dear too.'

Arabella had been poking at her hair and was sitting at the dressing-table, not saying much.

'Come and see the twins before we go downstairs. They're two months old—one of each. We are lucky, aren't we? A splendid start to the family.'

They were asleep—the little girl with mousy hair like her mother, the boy very fair. 'They're very good,' said their proud mother, 'and we've a wonderful nanny—my old housekeeper's niece.'

She led the way downstairs and into the drawing-room. 'Forgive me for talking so much, but I'm so glad to meet you. I've English friends, of course, but most of them live in Friesland—we've another house there...'

The room was warm and bright, with a brisk open fire and furnished with a nice mixture of antique furniture and comfortable chairs.

Titus got up as they came in, and the two dogs with him, staying politely on their feet until the three of them were seated and then collapsing into contented furry heaps before the fire. They talked over their coffee. It seemed that Titus knew many of the van der Linuses' friends and there was cheerful talk about St Nicolaas. 'I wish you could be here for that,' said Cressida. 'It's such fun for the children.' She jumped to her feet. 'Here's Aldrik...'

Arabella took to him at once. He was a year or two younger than Titus and his hair was already flecked with grey, but he was a handsome man—very tall and broad. He kissed his wife, then shook Titus's hand and smiled down at Arabella. 'I'm only sorry this is to be such a short visit,' he told her. 'Titus must bring you over for a week or two and come up to Friesland. That is our real home.'

Arabella thought privately that the one they were in now would do very nicely. 'Don't you work here?' she asked.

'Yes, but not all the time. Have you seen the twins?'

'Yes, they're adorable.'

He gave his wife a loving glance. 'We think so.' He went to sit down by Titus. 'There's a paper being read on asthma this afternoon. Do you care to come?'

They didn't linger over lunch and the men went away as soon as it was finished so, since it was a fine cold afternoon, the babies were wrapped up warmly, tucked into their pram and taken for a walk. They had been fed and played with and now they slept while the two girls gossiped. It struck Arabella that she had missed that during the last few months—cheerful chatter about clothes and husbands and babies, all of it light-hearted. They went back to tea and then to the nursery to help Nanny bath the twins, feed them once more and tuck them up in their cots. The men came home then, to pay a visit to the babies, which meant lifting them out of their cots while Nanny clucked her disapproval. Not that they minded—they made small contented noises into their father's broad shoulder and had no objection when they were passed to Titus.

Arabella, changing for dinner, hummed a little tune as she dressed. This was a happy household and the babies were delightful. It would be nice . . . She wasn't going to think about that, she told herself resolutely, and went downstairs to drink her sherry and enjoy the roast pheasant and red cabbage, game chips and roasted parsnips. It was beautfully cooked and served in the splendour of starched linen and silver, delicate china and crystal glasses.

The seminar started at eight o'clock in the morning and although they all breakfasted together the two men wasted no time over it. Aldrik gave his wife a lingering kiss and Titus pecked Arabella's cheek with a cheerful, 'See you later, Arabella.'

Cressida noticed that out of the corner of her eye and checked a small doubt. It was obvious that Titus and Arabella got on well together, were at ease with each other, but there was something missing . . .

'After I've fed the babies at ten o'clock would you like to come into the town and see the shops? They are not bad at all although I go to den Haag for my clothes. I do like that suit . . .'

It was as they were having their lunch that Aldrik phoned to say that he was bringing Dr Tulsma to dinner. 'She met Titus last time he was over here, darling, and shares his interest in long-term medication. I'm sorry—I know you don't like her but she more or less invited herself and Titus seemed quite enthusiastic. It's a subject dear to him, you know.'

'Well, there's nothing to do about it, is there, darling? Only don't let her stay to all hours.'

'We'll be back around six o'clock. Are you having a pleasant day with Arabella? Are the babies all right?'

'I'm enjoying myself very much; she's a dear and the babies are fine.'

'Darling,' said Aldrik, and rang off.

'There's someone coming to dinner,' said Cressida. 'A doctor—she's frightfully clever and she'll talk about enzymes and antibodies and things. She's invited herself and I'm sorry—I was looking forward to a chatty evening. If she suggests coming again I'll say we're going out for the evening.'

They spent a lazy afternoon and after tea bathed the babies and put them to bed since it was Nanny's evening off, and then they changed. Arabella, going through the clothes she had brought with her, decided on the jersey dress. Simple, beautiful material and worth every penny she had paid for it. Doing her hair, she decided that when she got back home she would go to a good hairdresser and have a perm, even have it all cut off—anything as long as it was different from the mousy topknot she was now arranging so neatly.

She and Cressida were in the drawing-room when the men got back.

Aldrik opened the door with a cheerful hello and stood back to allow a young woman to walk past him.

Cressida hadn't said what she was like—arrestingly handsome, with large blue eyes and corn-coloured hair in little curls all over her head, and her dress, of some flowing silky stuff, was cut low over an opulent bosom. She didn't look in the least like a doctor but vaguely romantic and mysterious. Arabella, being introduced, smiled and held out a hand. The enemy, she thought silently, and wondered why she had thought that.

Titus had smiled at her as he came into the room but that was all. She felt resentment bubbling up and suppressed it; later she would give it full rein... 'How delightful to meet you,' said Arabella mendaciously. 'What interesting work you do, and you and Titus share a common interest, don't you?' She sat down on a small sofa and patted the place beside her. 'Do sit down and tell me something about it. Have you known Titus a very long time?'

Geraldine Tulsma eyed her carefully. 'On and off for several years. You and Titus haven't been married long, have you?'

'No—but of course we've been friends for some time.' Arabella spoke airily. 'You're not married? Titus says you're very clever.'

Aldrik had given them their drinks and Arabella settled against the cushions, aware that the dress was falling in very satisfactory folds around her person. After all, that was what she had paid for...

'No, I'm not married. I have refused offers of marriage many times; my work is very important to me.' She spoke sharply. Here was this plain girl asking her patronising questions. 'Has Titus never spoken of me to you?'

'Well, no. What I mean is, I dare say he might have mentioned you—just to remark on your cleverness, you know. We have so many shared interests—nothing to do with his work or hospital.'

'I have come this evening so that I may continue to exchange views with Titus.'

'What a good idea. It's a pity you don't see more of each other.' She looked up as Cressida joined them.

'Getting to know each other?' she wanted to know. 'I'm sorry we haven't got a man for you, Geraldine, but it was such short notice.'

'I do not mind. It is Titus I wish to talk to.'

'Very well, why not? But shall we dine first?'

Arabella ate asparagus, coq au vin and chocolate and orange mousse piled high with whipped cream, and it all tasted the same—of nothing. Her keen dislike of Geraldine had taken away her appetite although she talked and laughed as everyone else did. Geraldine tended to carry on in a tedious fashion about herself, her aims and her ambitions and theories. They went back to the drawing-room for coffee and presently Geraldine suggested that she and Titus should have a quiet talk.

Arabella overheard her. 'I'm sure Titus is anxious to hear your views.' She gave him a smile as bright as a dagger's edge and he blinked at it before saying smoothly,

'Indeed I am, if you don't mind, Cressida? We don't want to inflict medical matters upon you.'

'Use my study,' said Aldrik. 'There'll be more coffee presently.'

When they had gone Cressida went up to the nursery to make sure that the twins were sleeping. 'I'm sorry that Geraldine invited herself here this evening,' said

Aldrik, 'she's heavy-going.' He glanced at his watch.
'I'll suggest driving her back as soon as we've had
some more coffee.'

'It's very nice,' said Arabella carefully, 'that Titus
has met someone he enjoys talking to. I mean, I don't
know anything about hospitals and medicine . . .'

'Nor does Cressida—you have no idea what a
blessing and a joy it is to come home each evening to
someone who doesn't know ichthyosis from nettle-
rash . . .'

'I do know what nettle-rash is!' said Arabella. They
were laughing about that as Titus and Geraldine came
back into the room and Aldrik rang for more coffee.

Cressida came back and they sat around drinking
it, chatting idly until Aldrik said, 'Isn't it time you
saw to the twins, my love? I'll run Geraldine back
home while you're doing that.'

'Don't bother,' said Geraldine. 'I've already asked
Titus to drive me back. We can finish our discussion—there hasn't been enough time . . .'

Titus put down his cup. 'Then, shall we go?' he
enquired mildly. 'We start early tomorrow morning,
do we not?'

'Such a pity that you are only here for such a short
time,' declared Geraldine in her rather loud voice. 'We
really should meet more often . . .'

A little imp of mischief took over from Arabella.
'Then why don't you come and visit us?' she asked,
and smiled at Titus. 'Wouldn't that be a good idea,
Titus?'

His face was inscrutable; she had no idea if he was
pleased or not. 'Oh, splendid,' he said. 'Shall we be
going, then?'

Geraldine pecked the air above Cressida's cheek, offered a hand to Arabella and said, '*Tot ziens*,' to the room at large.

'See you all later,' said Titus as he followed her out.

Cressida and Aldrik went to the door with them and Arabella went to the window. The light from the hall streamed out into the street and she could see Titus and Geraldine standing by the car, holding a conversation in which she took no part, laughing at some joke which she couldn't hear.

The enemy, thought Arabella. Geraldine was modern to her fingertips, attractive and determined— divorce would mean nothing to her and Titus was a prize worth having. I'm exaggerating, thought Arabella, and why do I feel like this about her? It isn't as if I love Titus. She caught her breath, because of course that wasn't true. She did love him; she was in love with him. She closed her eyes for a moment and when she opened them the car had gone. A good thing too, she reflected, for I might have gone outside and thumped Geraldine and flung myself at Titus.

She wanted to cry at the hopelessness of it all. Instead she stitched a smile on to her face and turned to make some cheerful remark to Cressida, unaware that she was as white as a sheet and trembling.

CHAPTER SEVEN

CRESSIDA was on the point of asking Arabella if she felt ill but Aldrik touched her arm and said cheerfully, 'Come over to the fire, Arabella. We're going to have another cup of coffee—do have one too.'

He began to talk about the evening and then the various lectures and the seminar he and Titus were to attend. 'Next year it will be held in London and so we shall see something of you there.'

'You must come and stay.' Arabella had pulled herself together. 'We shall love to have you and the babies, of course.'

They sat for half an hour or so and since there was no sign of Titus Arabella went to bed, to lie awake until she heard Titus's tread long after midnight. This is a pretty kettle of fish, she told herself. Of course, now she thought about it, she had been falling in love with Titus for weeks only she hadn't realised it. Would it have helped if she had known that before he had asked her to marry him? she wondered. She would have refused; being married to someone who didn't love you when you loved them would be an unbearable state in which to live. One in which she now found herself. But there is no reason, she reflected, why I shouldn't have a try at getting him to fall in love with me. The right make-up, a good hairdresser, attractive clothes, sparkling conversation and her feelings disguised under a friendly manner—but not too friendly. He must never think that she was trying to attract his attention or that she had no other interest in life but him.

A few tears escaped and trickled down her cheeks and she wiped them away impatiently. If she was to get the better of Geraldine and her like tears would be of no use. Suddenly full of determination to get the better of the enemy, Arabella went to sleep.

The men had already breakfasted and gone when she went down to breakfast with Cressida. 'I've been awake for hours,' said Cressida pouring their coffee. 'Aldrik read his paper to me—he always does, not that I understand any of it. He says it will bring him luck, not that he needs it. Did Titus wake you up to listen to his paper?' She didn't wait for an answer. 'We're a captive audience, aren't we?'

'I expect he's breaking me in gently,' said Arabella lightly. 'Do the twins let you sleep all night?'

'Oh, yes. Once or twice I've had to feed them in the small hours but now they're bigger they usually sleep right through until six o'clock. Aldrik's awfully good—we don't disturb Nanny and by the time they've settled the morning tea arrives.' She poured more coffee. 'Tell me, what did you think of Geraldine?' She grinned. 'You don't need to be polite.'

Arabella buttered some toast. 'I didn't like her. Far too handsome for one thing and so pleased with herself. All that bosom too...'

Cressida laughed. 'Frightful, isn't she? She's brilliantly clever, though. Aldrik can't stand her but even he admits that he admires her brain.' She glanced at Arabella. 'Did Titus give you his opinion? She kept him long enough—we heard him come in last night.'

'Yes, he was very late—I do hope he didn't disturb you.' She added for good measure, 'He was far too tired to talk about her.'

'You'll get the lot—chapter and verse. That's what's so nice about being married, telling each other things you would never dream of telling anyone else.'

Arabella agreed so quietly that Cressida made haste to talk about something else. 'If you would like to go sightseeing Nanny will have the twins until lunchtime. We might take a look round the town—there's the university and the Pieterskerk and the Rapenburg Canal. We can see the hospital from there too. There's Breestraat and the Town Hall and the St Anna Almshouses...'

'All in one morning?'

'Well, it will be a quick peek here and there but better than nothing. We must find time for coffee at Rotisserie Oude Leyden too...'

The morning was passed pleasantly and rather to their surprise the men came home for lunch.

'We didn't expect you,' said Cressida, lifting her face for a kiss. 'But now you're here we're very pleased.'

'We decided that the whole day without seeing either of you would be too long. What have you done with yourselves?'

They came home again soon after six o'clock that evening, and without Geraldine. Arabella, curling up in bed that night, thought with pleasure of the cosy evening—a delightful dinner and then sitting round the fire in the drawing-room talking about everything under the sun. Titus had kissed her with a sudden and unexpected warmth when she had gone upstairs with Cressida. Of course it might have been because the others were there watching them but she didn't think that he would pretend to something he didn't feel. They were going out on the following evening, she remembered sleepily. She would wear one of her new dresses ...

She was glad that she had chosen to wear the pink dress for they drove to den Haag where they dined at the Bistroquet—small and exclusive and, she guessed, wildly expensive. Afterwards they went to Scheveningen, to the Steigenberger Kurhaus, to dance and visit the casino. Titus had bought her some chips and she had tried her luck and won, and so had Cressida. She would have liked to put her winnings back on the table but the men had swept them back to dance. It had been a lovely evening and she had spent a good deal of it in Titus's arms dancing and, just for the moment, happy.

The next day was their last, with a formal banquet in the evening, and Arabella was glad that she had packed the green velvet. Inspecting her person before she went downstairs to join the others, she decided that she looked like a consultant's wife. She wished that Titus had given her a necklace as she fastened the double row of pearls her father had given to her on her eighteenth birthday. They were good ones and of course her engagement ring was everything a girl could wish for ...

'Oh, very nice,' said Cressida as she went into the drawing-room. She looked quite delightful herself in a smoky grey taffeta dress. She wore a diamond necklace and an exquisite bracelet—Arabella caught a glimpse of them as Aldrik wrapped her lovingly in an angora wrap.

Titus held her evening cloak with the impersonal courtesy which he might have afforded an elderly aunt... Arabella, suddenly angry, thanked him politely, her cheeks pink. He might at least pretend.

Titus, watching her from under his heavy lids, thought what a very pretty girl she had become in the few weeks of their marriage. It was the clothes, he supposed. When they got back to England he would look around for some jewellery for her. He felt a surge of delight at the sight of her and bent to kiss her cheek, an action which pleased Cressida, who, in the privacy of their bedroom, had informed Aldrik that their guests didn't behave in the least like a newly married couple.

'My dear love,' her husband had observed, 'you cannot judge others by our own experience. Probably they—er—let themselves go when they are alone, just as we do.'

The banquet was a grand affair and very formal. Arabella had never seen so many large elderly gentlemen in black ties, smoking cigars and tossing off tiny glasses of *genever*, nor had she seen so many dignified ladies with severe hairstyles and large bosoms encased in black satin. There were younger people there, of course, but they were swamped by the senior members of the university and the hospital. They were nice, she discovered, these self-assured dignitaries, and Titus seemed to know all of them. She was handed round and smiled at and patted and told how glad they were to see dear Dr Tavener married to such a charming little wife.

She sat next to a younger man at dinner, with an older man on her other side, both of whom made much of her so that her lovely eyes sparkled and her face glowed—not entirely with pleasure, though. Titus, she noted, had Geraldine on his right on the opposite side of the long table. Geraldine, she had to admit, looked strikingly handsome in peacock-blue chiffon. A pity there was to be no dancing, she reflected. As it was, they sat for a long time over dinner and then listened for even longer to a succession of speeches—some in English but most of them in Dutch. It was hard to maintain a look of interest. When they rose at last little groups were formed while, coffeecups or glasses in hand, people wandered from one to the other. The men were for the most part serious— swapping diagnoses, she supposed, listening with an air of great interest to an elderly professor detailing the history of the university to her.

It was as they were preparing to leave that she came face to face with Geraldine. 'Oh, there you are.' Her voice was patronising. 'I have hardly spoken to you all evening, have I?' She smiled in a self-satisfied manner and swirled the chiffon to show it to its best advantage. 'Titus and I have had a delightful evening—you don't mind, do you? We have known each other...'

Arabella interrupted her. 'Any friend of Titus's is a friend of mine,' she said sweetly, 'and do remember that we shall be delighted to see you if ever you come to England. Perhaps your work keeps you here, though?'

'No, no. I am well-known both in England and the States, as well as in Europe.' She gave a satisfied little laugh. 'I am free to take a holiday when I wish.'

'How nice,' said Arabella. 'It's been pleasant meeting you. We're going home tomorrow but of course Titus will have told you... So I'll say goodbye.'

Geraldine offered a hand. 'Shall we not say, *tot
ziens*? That means——'

'Yes, I know what it means. I must go—I can see
Cressida waiting for me.'

There was no sign of Titus. 'A good thing he came
in his own car,' said Cressida. 'He's driving Geraldine
back. Why that woman can't drive her own car beats
me—anyone would think that she had already
asked——' She stopped as Aldrik squeezed her arm.

'The trouble with Geraldine is that given an inch
she takes an ell.' He took Arabella's arm. 'Did you
enjoy your evening? It was all a bit serious, I'm
afraid.'

'I enjoyed myself,' said Arabella, her eyes sparkling
with temper. 'What a handsome lot of professors and
medical people you've got living here.'

'Indeed, yes. I have to keep a tight rein on Cressy
when we come to these gatherings; she's inclined to
fall for bearded professors!'

'If you ever grow a beard I shall leave you,' declared Cressida as they went out to the car. 'When we
get home I shall make a big pot of tea and we can
drink it in the kitchen while we tear the women's
dresses to pieces. There was one—you must have seen
it, Arabella—purple crushed velvet, very tight in the
wrong places ...'

On this light-hearted note the evening ended, but
although she sat for some time, drinking tea out of
mugs and discussing the evening, there was no sign
of Titus.

Arabella, with the excuse that she must do some
packing if they were to leave in time for the ferry in
the morning, went to bed, declaring that she hadn't

enjoyed herself so much for years. 'You must all come and stay soon,' she said. 'I shall miss you so.'

After she had gone Cressida collected up their mugs. 'Darling,' she began, 'there's something not quite right...'

'My love, Arabella and Titus are grown people.' He smiled. 'Somehow I don't think we need to worry. Arabella is no fool, Cressy.'

'Does that mean that Titus is?'

'No, no—we men are notoriously blind, love, as you well know.'

She skipped across the kitchen into his arms. 'I'd like them to be as happy as we are.'

Titus was at breakfast looking well rested and impeccably turned out. He and Aldrik had been out with the dogs and were in some deep discussion while Arabella and Cressida talked of Christmas and what they planned to do. Presently they went upstairs to see the babies and then it was time to go. The men had joined them in the nursery but time was running out. They made their final goodbyes, got into the car and drove to the Hoek, boarded the ferry and, in due course, landed at Harwich.

They were home that evening to be greeted by Mrs Turner, a great pile of letters for Titus and a number of messages on the answering machine. Titus, coming from his study just before they were to sit down to dinner, came into the drawing-room.

'I have to go to the hospital—it's a matter of some urgency. I'm sorry, Arabella. Please don't wait up if I'm not back. Tell Mrs Turner to lock up; I'll let myself in.'

'We'll leave something for you in the kitchen; it'll keep hot on the Aga. I hope it's nothing too serious and that you can put it right.'

He came across the room and bent to kiss her. 'What a perfect wife you are, Arabella. This does happen from time to time.'

'Well, it's bound to, isn't it?' she said in a matter of fact voice. 'Be sure and have something when you get back if we are all in bed.'

She listened to the street door closing and went to tell Mrs Turner, reflecting that a doctor's wife could expect this—and not just once but over and over again.

She ate her solitary dinner, thinking about him. He was everything a girl could wish for and she loved him—two reasons to strengthen her resolve to make him love her. He liked her and perhaps he felt affection for her—but that wouldn't do. She would have to do something to make him see her with different eyes—not just as a quiet companion, ready at hand to listen when he wanted to talk or walk, but as a girl to take him by surprise so that he really saw her.

He hadn't returned by eleven o'clock; Mrs Turner had already locked up so Arabella went to bed.

'Was it all right?' Arabella asked at breakfast. Titus was already at the table but he got up to pull out her chair. He looked as though he had had a good night's sleep but her loving eyes could see that he was tired. 'Were you up all night?'

'Until just after four o'clock this morning. He'll pull through.'

'I'm glad. It must make you feel good.'

He smiled. 'Yes, it does. I'll be at my rooms until this afternoon, then the hospital. I expect to be home soon after five o'clock.'

'Oh, good. Shall we have tea together?'

'That would be delightful. What are you going to do today?'

'Well—I thought I'd go to the hairdresser. I wondered if I had my hair cut short and permed——'

He said with surprising sharpness, 'No, Arabella, I like your hair just as it is—don't let anyone touch it. Have it washed as often as you like but not an inch of it must be cut off.'

She stared at him round-eyed. 'All right, Titus, then I won't. Only I thought it would improve my looks.'

'Your looks are very nice as they are.'

'Thank you. I thought you liked short curly hair and I wanted to please you.'

'Well, I don't and that reminds me—why in heaven's name did you ask Geraldine Tulsma to come and see us?'

She looked meek. 'Titus, I thought you liked her, and she told me that you were old friends. You spent a lot of time together...'

She spoke so artlessly that he sat back and looked at her thoughtfully. He smiled then. 'So we did. She's very attractive, isn't she? Apart from her brilliant brain.'

'She's almost beautiful and it must be nice to be able to talk about things and know the person you're talking to understands exactly what you're saying.' She took a breath. 'She would have made you a splendid wife, Titus—if I'd known about her...'

'An interesting thought, my dear.' He got up, patted her on the shoulder in what she felt was an avuncular fashion and said, 'I must be off. See you this evening.'

She telephoned the manor when he had gone and talked for a long time to old Mrs Tavener and then spoke to Butter, who assured her that the dogs and Percy were fine and that Bess and Jerry were full of spirit. 'Looking forward to seeing you, ma'am—coming for the weekend, I hope?'

'I do hope so, but I don't know if the doctor will be free. I want to talk about Christmas with Mrs Butter...'

'We'll hope to see you, ma'am.'

It would be nice to be at the manor again, she thought, and went to put on her outdoor things. She hadn't thought about Christmas presents—it might be a good idea to look round the shops and decide on what to buy. It would have been fun to have had Titus with her.

When he got home he asked her what she had been doing.

'Looking at the shop windows, trying to decide what to buy for Christmas presents,' she told him.

'I'll give myself a half-day tomorrow—in fact I had arranged it some time ago. We'll go shopping together.'

'Oh, Titus, how lovely. I've made a list...'

She didn't think she would ever forget their afternoon together. He parked the car in the forecourt of a hospital near the Brompton Road and walked her to Harrods to embark on the kind of shopping spree every woman would dream of. There were gloves for Miss Baird, a crimson dressing-gown for Mrs Turner, a charming tea-service for the Butters, a fine woollen stole for Miss Welling in rose-pink—to give her some colour, as Arabella said—the latest novels for Cressida, teething-rings for the twins, a hamper for Mr Flinn and a beautiful vase for the Marshalls.

'That takes care of the bulk,' said Titus. 'We give the nurses a bottle of wine and a cheque and the same for the maids and the gardener at the manor.'

'And the boy who helps in the garden?'

He smiled down at her. 'I happen to know that he wants football boots—he's in the village team. The men who come up to help had better have cash. Now we have to find something for Grandmother.'

The jeweller's shop was like an Aladdin's cave. 'What do you suppose she would like?' asked Titus.

'Something she can put on easily,' said Arabella very sensibly. 'And something she can wear each day if she wants to. A chain perhaps?'

They had looked at chains of all types and chosen a fairly long one of gold links with a gold tassel. It was a beautiful thing and just right for the old lady. While it was being wrapped up Arabella went from showcase to showcase, admiring their contents, but only to herself. Titus was a generous man—if she evinced a desire for a diamond necklace she had no doubt that he would buy it for her. That wasn't what she wanted, though. She would rather have a bag of apples he had bought for her without any hint on her part.

They went home presently and piled the parcels on the sitting-room table. 'I'll leave you to wrap them up,' said Titus easily. 'I'm sure you'll do it beautifully. They will keep you occupied tomorrow—I'm going to Birmingham to a consultation; I may stay the night.'

He looked at her as he spoke and she quickly arranged her features to an expression of interested concern. 'Would you like me to pack a bag for you? You'll drive there?'

'Yes—you won't be lonely?'

'Good gracious, no.' She had spoken too quickly and added, 'Not with all those presents to wrap up. Besides, I've still a few more presents to buy and what about the Christmas cards?'

They had chosen them and ordered them to be printed but she had no idea to whom they should be sent when they arrived.

'There is a list in the top right drawer of my desk in the study; you can safely send a card to each address on it. I usually get Miss Baird to do them but it would be much nicer if you were to sign them yourself for us both.'

'Very well. You will be free to go to the manor for Christmas?'

'Yes, unless something very urgent crops up. We'll go down next Saturday too, shall we?'

'Yes, please. It will be nice to see the animals again. Butter says they're all very well and happy and I talked to your grandmother—she was hoping you'd be free next weekend.'

He nodded. 'I've some work to do now—could dinner be put back for half an hour or so?'

'Of course. I'll go along and see Mrs Turner.' As they crossed the hall she said, 'It was a lovely afternoon, Titus, thank you for taking me.'

'I enjoyed it too.' He sounded remote.

In his study he didn't pick up the telephone immediately. It was quite true, he had enjoyed himself— perhaps because Arabella had been so obviously delighted with everything she saw. Her ordinary face under her charming hat had glowed with pleasure. She was, he decided, really a pretty girl and her new clothes had made no difference to her; she was still forthright and sensible and undemanding. A most agreeable person to live with and one he would miss—the very thought of that made him frown. Really he was getting quite fond of her.

His work forgotten, he allowed his thoughts to wander.

Arabella's thoughts were wandering too as she changed into one of her new dresses, but they wandered to some good purpose. Sternly suppressing her more loving thoughts of Titus, she concentrated them on the best way in which to encourage him to fall in love with her. Perhaps she was too much the taken-for-granted friend, rather like a favourite pair of comfortable shoes—hardly noticed but always there. A little coolness perhaps, a slight show of independence—although she had no idea how to set about that. Beyond his remarks that she looked nice from time to time, her beautiful new clothes hadn't had much effect upon him. It was a pity she couldn't alter her face. In the privacy of her room she had tried out various make-ups and decided that all of them made her look peculiar, and he had sounded annoyed when she had suggested that she should have her hair cut off.

'Oh, well,' said Arabella. 'I must leave Fate to take a hand.' She gave her hair a final pat and went down to the drawing-room.

Titus was still in his study but he joined her for dinner presently and spent the evening with her, talking idly about their plans for Christmas. There was an annual party for the children in the village, he explained, and they should attend. The carol singers would come early on Christmas Eve and be invited into the manor—a long-held custom.

Arabella nodded. 'Mince pies and hot drinks. Shall we have a Christmas tree?'

'Of course—Butter sees to that. There will be one or two of the family there.' When she looked up in surprise, for he had told her that his parents had been dead for some years, he said, 'An aunt or so—and a couple of cousins and their children. And a great-uncle to keep Grandmother amused...' He added gently, 'I didn't tell you before—I didn't want you to worry about meeting a number of strangers, but they are family; we meet seldom, but Christmas is a long-standing custom I don't care to break.'

'A house full of guests is lovely for Christmas,' said Arabella. 'It will be delightful to meet your family. If you'll give me a list of their names I'll look for presents...'

'Will you? I'm afraid I shan't have the time. We're not doing anything for the rest of the weekend, are we?'

'Just Dr and Mrs Marshall coming to dinner the day after tomorrow.'

'Ah, yes, of course.' He stretched out his long legs and picked up the newspaper.

'The week after next,' said Arabella in a no-nonsense voice, 'we are invited to a party at Mrs Lamb's. You told me to accept.'

'Oh, lord, I'd forgotten.' He looked at her over the paper. 'An indefatigable matchmaker on my behalf—she knew my mother well and seemed to think that it was her duty to find me a wife.'

'Oh, dear. Need I go? I could have a headache . . .'

'My dear girl, my main purpose in marrying you was to put a stop to Mrs Lamb's efforts to introduce me to those ladies whom she considered suitable.'

If that was meant as a compliment, thought Arabella, it had been rather ineptly put. She sighed. Not only had she to contend with Geraldine, the enemy, now there was Mrs Lamb too. She said merely, 'Is it a dress-up party?'

'Very much so. Black tie and long frocks. Buy something for it—you always look very nice.'

Who wants to look nice? thought Arabella and smiled sweetly at him.

She would find something to make him open his eyes—black velvet perhaps, with a tight skirt slit all the way up and a plunging neckline. She couldn't hope to compete with Geraldine but she had some nice curves.

Of course she didn't buy the black velvet, but a lengthy prowl at Harrods the next day brought to light the very dress she knew would be right for the occasion. Silver-grey chiffon over a satin slip, cunningly fashioned to emphasise and make the most of the curves. She studied herself in the long mirror in the fitting-room and nodded with satisfaction. It concealed what it revealed—or should that be the other way round? Anyway, it was a masterpiece and never mind the price.

Leaving the shop, the dress box in her hand, she felt guilty at spending money—so much money—when there were so many people who needed it so badly. She opened her purse and gave an elderly man selling cheap cigarettes and lighters its entire contents. She had to walk all the way home after that but at least she had made someone happy.

The cards had come and she went to Titus's study to look for the list he had told her to use. There was another list there too—charities, a dozen or more. She read it and felt a surge of love for him. He might have wealth but he was generous too. She sat down at his desk, in his big chair, and began on the Christmas cards.

The Marshalls came on Sunday evening. She and Mrs Turner had planned a special menu and she had set the table with lace mats and the silver and crystal and arranged a low bowl of holly and Christmas roses with silver candelabra on either side. They were to have watercress soup, rack of lamb and a mince tart with syllabub to follow. Arabella had itched to do the cooking but Mrs Turner's feelings would have been hurt. Besides, she was an excellent cook. Arabella went upstairs to shower and get into the silk jersey dress, well pleased with her preparations. Before she went downstairs she opened the closet door and took another look at the grey dress. It gave her a thrill just to look at it; she hoped that Titus would get a thrill too.

The evening was very successful; the Marshalls were good company and dinner was as good as she had hoped it would be. They had their coffee, idly gos-

siping in the drawing-room until the men went away
to Titus's study to discuss a case, leaving Arabella
and Mrs Marshall by the fire.

Mrs Marshall had known Titus for some years and
had frequently urged him to marry. Now, sitting opposite his wife, she felt satisfied that Arabella was the
right girl for him. No looks, of course, but charm and
a pretty voice, a good figure and lovely eyes. They
were easy in each other's company too, almost like
very old friends. There were none of those sidelong
loving glances she would have expected from
newlyweds, although of course Titus wasn't a man to
show his feelings and she didn't think Arabella would
either. She began to talk about Mrs Lamb's party,
an annual event which was always a success. 'You'll
enjoy every minute of it,' she assured Arabella,
happily unaware how wildly awry this statement would
prove to be.

Arabella and Titus drove down to the manor on the
following Saturday morning. It was a cold grey day
but the house looked welcoming and as he stopped
the car the door was opened by Butter and all three
dogs came pelting out to greet them. Percy, more
prudent and disliking the cold weather, had stationed
himself in the hall and Arabella, making much of all
four of them, turned a beaming face to Titus.

'Oh, it is nice to be home.' She paused. 'What I
mean is, London's home too, but this is different,
isn't it?'

'I know what you mean. Let Butter have your
things, we'll go and see Grandmother, shall we?'

Mrs Tavener was in her room, sitting very upright
beside the fire while Miss Welling read to her. She

looked round as they came in, Percy in Arabella's arms, the dogs at their heels.

'My dears—how delightful to see you. Miss Welling, fetch the sherry—we must all drink to this happy meeting.'

Which they did, while they told her about Leiden— Arabella doing most of the talking while Titus sat, watching her, putting in a word here and there. The day went too fast after that and so did Sunday. They got into the car after tea, this time with Beauty and Bassett—Percy was to stay at the manor since he and Duke had become firm friends.

'We will be down again next weekend,' said Titus, eyeing her downcast face. 'If you would like to do so, there is no reason why you shouldn't stay for a week or two after Christmas.'

She spoke without thinking. 'And leave you alone in London? I couldn't do that.'

He turned to look at her but she was gazing out of the window.

He was away very early on Monday morning to take a teaching round, leaving her to finish the cards and buy the rest of the presents. When he got home in the evening she saw that he was tired. She gave him a second look—not tired perhaps, but worried about something. And when he wanted to know how she had spent her day she told him in her quiet voice.

His eyes were on her face. 'How restful you are, Arabella,' he observed, and when she looked up, surprised, he asked, 'Have the dogs been good?'

The party was the next day. Anxious to look her best, she creamed her face, did her nails, washed her hair and took another look at the dress.

When the day arrived she bade him goodbye after they had had breakfast and assured him that she would have a late tea ready for him before they needed to dress, and then she went off to the kitchen to talk to Mrs Turner and take the dogs for their romp in the garden. Glowing from the cold air, back indoors, she went upstairs to Titus's room to lay out his clothes for the evening only to be interrupted by a peal on the doorbell. She was at the head of the staircase when Mrs Turner opened the door and after a moment stood aside to admit someone. Geraldine Tulsma.

Arabella, hurrying down to the hall, saw that she had a suitcase with her and her heart sank.

Geraldine was in complete command of the situation. 'Here I am, Arabella. I have a day or two free and I know Titus will be delighted to see me.' She shook hands. 'We have known each other too long to stand on ceremony.'

'He's at the hospital,' said Arabella and added belatedly, 'How nice to see you, Geraldine.'

'He'll be home for lunch?'

Arabella led the way into the drawing room. 'Well, no, he won't be back until about five o'clock—we're going to a party this evening . . .'

'I'll come with you. We're bound to get a chance to talk there—you know what parties are, all noise and chatter, ideal for a quiet discussion. There's a theory I intend to tell him about . . .'

'How nice,' said Arabella, and felt foolish. 'Do sit down and have some coffee. I'll tell Mrs Turner to get a room ready for you.'

It was like being in a bad dream. Geraldine might despise her as a woman but Arabella was an audience; her ears were ringing by the end of the afternoon.

Geraldine had a splendid opinion of herself and liked people to know it.

I don't think Titus will be pleased, thought Arabella as she heard the front door being opened.

CHAPTER EIGHT

ARABELLA got up and went into the hall, anxious to tell Titus that Geraldine was there, but Geraldine came with her, hurrying past her and taking Titus's hand in hers.

'I've surprised you,' she exclaimed in her vibrant tones. 'I have a few days off and I came at once, knowing that you would be delighted to talk to someone with a mind compatible with your own.'

The doctor shook the hand on his arm and handed it back. Looking at him, there was no knowing what his feelings might be. He said pleasantly, 'This is indeed a surprise, Geraldine.'

'I knew that you would be delighted.' She waited impatiently as he crossed the hall to kiss Arabella's cheek. 'I hear there's a party tonight. I'm sure no one will mind if I come along too.'

Arabella found her voice and was pleased to hear how pleasant it sounded. 'I'll phone, shall I, Titus? I'm sure Geraldine will be welcome. After all, there will be so many people there that one more won't be noticed.'

He hid a smile. 'Yes, by all means do that, my dear. Now, if you will forgive me I have some phoning to do. I'll be in my study if you should want me, Arabella.'

Geraldine looked disappointed. 'I suppose it is necessary for him to go away,' she observed to

Arabella. 'I will go to my room and unpack and rest until he has finished what he has to do.'

Arabella, the epitome of the perfect hostess, led the way upstairs, offered refreshment, an extra blanket and the assurance that she would be waiting to let Geraldine know the moment that Titus was free.

'I hope those dogs will be quiet,' said Geraldine. 'I do not care for them. And you have a cat...'

'Yes,' said Arabella equably, 'we both like animals.'

She went downstairs, her eyes sparkling with rage. It wouldn't have mattered so much if Titus had looked annoyed, even taken aback at Geraldine's appearance. There had been no expression on his face—— She paused. Yes, there had. Faint amusement. She couldn't think why.

She went to the phone then, to explain about their unexpected guest, and was assured that their hostess would be delighted to see any friend of Titus's. 'Friend,' muttered Arabella through her teeth, and turned to find Titus in the doorway, watching her.

'Geraldine's very welcome,' she told him airily. 'I'll just go and talk to Mrs Turner.'

That lady's feathers were ruffled—the nice little dinner for two would have to be stretched to three. 'Coming unexpected like that,' she grumbled to Arabella. 'How long will she be stopping, ma'am?'

'Well, not long, I think. She said something about a few days...'

Mrs Turner gave the sauce she was stirring a look which should have curdled it.

Titus was in the drawing-room when she went back there, stretched out in his armchair with Percy on his knee and the dogs drowsing by the fire. Arabella eyed him peevishly. 'I'll go and tell Geraldine that you're

out of the study—she asked me to let her know. I'm
sure you won't want to miss any time with her!'

She flounced to the door to be halted by his quiet
voice. 'Am I mistaken in thinking that you are making
it as easy as possible for Geraldine and me to be
together, Arabella?'

'Well, that's what you want, isn't it? I hadn't
noticed you discouraging her.' She swept out of the
room and went to tap on their guest's door.

Dressing for the party, Arabella reflected that if
Titus and Geraldine had wanted to be together she
had given them every opportunity. After a token appearance with their guest she had excused herself on
some household pretext and left them alone. 'And I
hope they enjoy each other's society,' she observed to
Percy, sitting on the end of her bed, watching her as
she dressed.

Contrary to the normal desires of a woman in love,
Arabella ignored the silver-grey dress and picked out
a dress which hadn't been designed to catch a man's
eye at all—an elegant mouse-brown silk crêpe,
guaranteed to be eclipsed by the other gowns worn at
the party. She had overlooked the fact that it fitted
her quite delightfully and by its very quiet elegance
would stand out in a crowd.

Her hair in a french pleat, her face nicely made up,
she went down to the drawing-room to find Titus
already there. He got up when she went in and took
stock of her. 'Charming.' He took a box from his
pocket. 'I would like you to wear this, Arabella...'

He had gently unclasped the pearls around her neck
and fastened a diamond necklace in its place. He
didn't say anything and after a moment she crossed
to the great mirror over the fireplace and took a look.

It was a delicate affair, the diamonds set in small flower-like sprays in gold, the necklace a series of fine gold loops between each spray. It looked like a spangled spider's web. She touched it gently. 'It's old . . .'

'Yes. It has been in the family for a great many years and is handed down from one bride to the next.'

She looked at his reflection in the mirror. 'So of course it is right and proper that your wife should wear it this evening.' She turned on him, her cheeks very pink. 'We have to keep up appearances, do we not?'

He had gone rather white. 'If that is how you choose to look at it . . .'

The door opened and Geraldine came in, wearing another floating chiffon creation in vivid pink.

'What a charming dress,' said Arabella. 'So—so colourful, don't you agree, Titus?'

'Extremely so.'

Geraldine viewed her opulent person with satisfaction. 'One doesn't want to look drab...' She smiled at Arabella. 'Time enough to dress in brown and black and grey when one is old. Are we likely to meet anyone interesting this evening?'

'I'm sure you will meet someone to interest you,' said Titus smoothly.

Arabella added sweetly, 'You can always fall back on Titus.'

A remark which earned her a cold stare from her husband.

The party was in full swing when they arrived. Arabella, Titus's firm hand steering her from group to group, smiled and shook hands and murmured party talk, all the while aware that breathing down

her neck was Geraldine, intent on keeping as close to
Titus as possible. If he minded this, there was no sign
of it and presently, after the dancing had started and
he had had the first dance with Arabella, he handed
her over to an eager young man and as she danced
away she saw him bending his head to hear what
Geraldine was saying.

She saw them dancing together presently and then
lost sight of them as she went from one partner to the
other—a small graceful girl, the brown dress a
splendid foil for the diamonds around her neck.

There was a buffet supper and briefly she found
Titus with her again but, since there were half a dozen
other people clustered around the table, talking was
out of the question—besides, what did she have to
say?

She danced for the rest of the evening while she
laughed and talked and wondered if Titus would ever
fall in love with her. Several of the men there had
expressed their pleasure in her company, which was
more, she reflected unfairly, than Titus had ever done.
Memory could be a very convenient thing to lose when
one was angry and unhappy and, she had to admit,
jealous of the tiresome Geraldine.

Back at the house in the very early hours of the
morning, that lady showed an alarming tendency to
sit about discussing the evening. Arabella wondered
what she should do. Urge the lady to go to bed? Go
to bed herself and leave her with Titus? Make some
graceful remark and sweep Geraldine upstairs with
her? She might not go...

It was Titus who said presently, 'Well, I've some
work to finish. I'll say goodnight, Geraldine.' He

kissed Arabella very deliberately. 'I won't disturb you, my dear.'

Arabella saw Geraldine's instantly alert face. 'Oh, I'm a light sleeper, Titus—I dare say I'll still be awake,' she uttered in a voice dripping with sweetness while she glared at him.

Percy was at the top of the stairs, waiting for her. 'I believe cats to be dirty animals,' said Geraldine, sweeping past him.

'Have you ever watched a cat washing itself? A pity some humans aren't as thorough.' Arabella saw her guest to her bedroom door, wished her goodnight and, gathering up Percy, went to her own room.

The house was very quiet. She undressed, put on her dressing-gown and, bidding Percy stay where he was on the bed, tiptoed downstairs again. Bassett and Beauty would be in the kitchen; she always went to see them before she went to bed.

They were snoozing in their baskets but they woke as she went into the warm room. She bade them goodnight, sitting on the floor between them, an arm round Bassett's small body and the other around Beauty's massive neck. The day had been horrid and she was glad it was all over.

'Though mind you,' said Arabella, 'tomorrow may be a great deal worse.'

Presently she crept back through the house and up the stairs, unaware that Titus had opened his study door and was watching her.

Titus was getting ready to leave the house when she went down to breakfast. 'Geraldine not with you?' he wanted to know.

'She fancied breakfast in bed,' said Arabella, matter-of-factly. 'Did you want to see her? Shall I give her a message?'

His look made her feel uncomfortable. Was it amusement? What had he to be amused about?

'Would you tell her that I have arranged a visit to the Royal College of Physicians? Eleven o'clock—the main door. I'll be home some time after five o'clock, Arabella.' He turned at the door. 'Did I tell you how charming you looked last night?'

He had gone before she could think of a reply to that, which was as well for she was fuming at the thought of him and Geraldine strolling round the Royal College of Physicians. She was vague as to what functions were held there or for what purpose one would visit it—sufficient that the pair of them were going to spend the morning there and probably have lunch together afterwards...

She went upstairs to give Geraldine the message, noting with satisfaction that while her guest when fully clothed gave the appearance of a magnificent figure, in bed she was plain fat. She probably wore a strongly built foundation with bones...

'I shall be out to lunch,' said Geraldine, without bothering to thank Arabella for the message. She took a bite of toast. 'Titus enjoys my company.' She slid a sly glance in Arabella's direction. 'But of course you know about that.'

Arabella sat down in a pretty little armchair by the window. 'No, I don't—at least, not your version. Do tell?'

'Many men have loved me,' declared Geraldine smugly, 'but there is only one whom I wish to marry and that is Titus—he must have told you that he

wanted to marry me?' She didn't wait for an answer,
which was just as well. 'But I was a silly girl. I wished
to make my mark in the medical world and so I con-
tinued to refuse him—each time he came to Leiden I
would say no. I was wrong, of course—two brilliant
minds such as ours are meant to become one. I cannot
blame him for marrying you—there is nothing about
you which could come between us. You are of no account; you are not clever, nor are you pretty. A very
nice person, I am sure,' she added graciously,
'therefore I have no feelings of jealousy about you.
You are Titus's wife but of course he has no love for
you, that is obvious to my eyes—the eyes of a woman
who loves him.'

Arabella found her voice. She could stand no more.
'How very interesting—but I mustn't keep you talking
or you will be late. Have you finished your breakfast?
I'll take the tray. Mrs Turner is busy and I'm going
downstairs anyway.' She added politely, 'Do you know
how to get to this place.'

'No.'

'No, nor do I. I should take a taxi or ask a
policeman.'

She was in the garden with Percy and the dogs when
Geraldine called to say, 'I am going now,' and added,
'I shall be back during the afternoon.'

Arabella went to the front door with her, wished
her a delightful day and closed the door after her. She
would feel better if she had a nice quiet cry. She leaned
against the door and sniffed and snivelled and sobbed,
and then went and washed her face, powdered her
pink nose and drank the coffee Mrs Turner brought
her, carefully avoiding looking at her swollen eyes and
ill-disguised nose.

'That woman,' said Mrs Turner viciously to Betty, one of the girls who came in daily to help. 'I'd like to get my hands on her. The doctor must be out of his mind. And don't you remember what I've just said, or breathe a word, or I'll take my rolling pin to you!'

Arabella took the dogs into the park and came back for lunch, which she pushed around her plate and didn't eat. There was no sign of Geraldine but she hadn't expected there to be. She got into her outdoor things again, told Mrs Turner that she was going shopping and would be back for tea, and let herself out of the house.

She had no idea where she wanted to go. A cruising taxi came along and she hailed it and said, 'Oxford Street,' because it was the first place she thought of. There were lights there and the pavements were thronged with people doing their Christmas shopping. She walked slowly, stopping to look at the gaily dressed windows, buying several things she neither needed nor liked particularly—a scarf which was of a colour she never wore, socks with Father Christmas and his reindeer embroidered on them, which Titus would receive with outward pleasure and never wear and a pair of outsize earrings, glittering with imitation jewels, dangling almost to her shoulders. When she got home she put them all carefully in a drawer in her bedroom. The scarf at least would be just right for Betty, who loved bright colours. The socks she buried under a pile of undies but the earrings she put on. They looked absurd and she turned her head to and fro watching them swing and glitter. She kept them on and went downstairs to have her tea in the animals' company.

Mrs Turner brought the tea tray. 'That Dr Tulsma came back an hour ago. Said she needed to rest. Shall I tell her the tea's ready?'

'Please, Mrs Turner.'

Geraldine joined her five minutes later and Arabella handed her her tea, offered the cakes and enquired as to her day.

'A splendid day,' said Geraldine loudly. 'I have never enjoyed myself so much—so much to talk about and a delicious lunch. I do not know how I am going to tear myself away from you...'

'Oh, do you have to go back shortly?' Arabella did her best not to sound delighted.

'My dear Arabella, duty calls and someone in my position cannot ignore that. I go on an evening flight. I rang for a taxi just before you returned home.'

'Rang for a taxi?' repeated Arabella. 'You mean you're on the point of leaving now?'

'Indeed I am.' She glanced at the clock. 'In ten minutes or so.'

'Can't you wait for Titus? He'll be so disappointed and I'm sure he would drive you to Heathrow.'

Geraldine put her hand on her ample bosom. 'We have said goodbye. We have to be satisfied with these brief glimpses of each other—there will be other meetings.'

She went away to fetch her things and Arabella, rather dazed with the suddenness of it all, wished her goodbye and a safe journey.

'You are quite a nice little thing,' said Geraldine. 'I can understand that Titus finds you exactly the kind of wife he needs—undemanding and allowing him to lead his own life and lacking in childish romantic notions. Goodbye, Arabella.'

She went out to the waiting taxi and Arabella shut the door on her for the second time that day. Mrs Turner, coming into the hall, took a look at her face. 'I'll make a nice pot of tea, ma'am, and you just sit down and enjoy it. It's not my place to say so, but it's nice to have the house quiet once more.'

'She's very beautiful,' said Arabella in a small voice.

'Beauty is but skin-deep,' quoth Mrs Turner. 'Just you go back and sit by the fire and there'll be a fresh pot of tea in a brace of shakes.'

Arabella drank the tea and then sat back in her chair, Percy on her knee, the two dogs sprawled at her feet. The day's happenings had been strange and they had sounded the death knell over any hopes she might have had about Titus's feelings towards her. Geraldine had made it clear that she and Titus would have married save for her reluctance to give up her career, and although Arabella hated her she couldn't believe that she would tell a pack of deliberate lies about it. Titus had made it plain before they married that although she and he were friends there was no question of love.

She was still sitting there, the tea forgotten, when Titus came in. It was unfortunate that the first thing he said was, 'Hello, where's Geraldine?'

Arabella sat up straight; the dogs had run to meet him and Percy set indignant claws in her skirt at being disturbed. 'She left for Heathrow half an hour ago.'

He sat down opposite her. 'Rather unexpected— did she get a phone call to return, I wonder?'

Arabella said carefully, 'You don't need to pretend, Titus. She told me about you and her. You said goodbye this afternoon after you'd had lunch together, didn't you? You knew she was going back.'

She swallowed the lump of tears in her throat. 'I'm only sorry that you must both be so unhappy. Of course it can all be put right, can't it? It's easy these days and it isn't as if...'

'Before you go on with this rigmarole, Arabella, let us put it into plain language.'

He had spoken quietly but his voice was cold and his eyes, when she looked at him, were hard and cold. 'Not to mince matters, you are telling me that Geraldine and I are in love, that we are unhappy and you are kindly planning to divorce me.'

'Well, that's what I said, didn't I? It was plain enough for an idiot to understand. I can quite see that you need a wife—I suppose all professional men do—but why pick on me?' She answered herself. 'I'm un-demanding and allow you to lead your own life and I don't have any childish romantic notions—she told me that.'

'Did she, indeed? Geraldine seems to have told you a great deal. And you believed her?'

'I didn't want to, really I didn't, but someone like her—I mean, an important well-known doctor wouldn't tell lies, would she? Besides, you said that you wished to marry for the wrong reasons—for someone to come home to each day, a companion, someone to put an end to your friends trying to marry you off. I accepted all that but only because I didn't know about Geraldine, did I?'

'You don't want to hear my side of the story?'

'I wouldn't be human if I didn't, would I? But I don't want to—I'm sure talking about it would make you feel unhappy.'

'Not unhappy, my dear Arabella, but blind with rage, and if you persist in sitting there filled with sweetness and forgiveness I shall wring your little neck.'

'In that case,' said Arabella, 'I shall go and sit somewhere else.'

She whisked out of the room, clutching Percy, and went to the kitchen to say that she had a headache and would go to bed.

'A morsel of supper?' asked Mrs Turner.

'No—no, thank you. The doctor will dine at the usual time, please.'

The doctor had poured himself a drink and gone back to his chair. He sat for a long time deep in thought, but presently he laughed. 'What a pair of fools we are,' he observed to the dogs, who mumbled an understanding and went to sleep again.

'Madam's gone to her bed,' said Mrs Turner severely, serving him his soup. 'Got a headache and I'm not surprised. I may be speaking out of turn, sir, but that ladyfriend of yours fair upset madam.'

The doctor tasted his soup. 'Delicious. Dr Tulsma and Mrs Tavener don't have much in common, Mrs Turner, and her visit was unexpected.' He glanced up at his faithful housekeeper. 'I think it unlikely that she will visit us again.'

'That's a good thing, sir, for I don't like to see madam upset—such a sweet little lady she is, as you well know, no doubt.'

'No doubt at all. Will you take a nice little supper upstairs presently? A little food often helps a headache.'

'One of my omelettes,' breathed Mrs Turner, and went back to the kitchen with his soup plate.

Arabella, fortified by a delicious light supper, slept soundly and went down to breakfast. She had no wish to apologise and indeed she couldn't see why she should—he had wanted to wring her neck, hadn't he? He was the one to apologise. She sat down opposite him at the breakfast table and poured herself a cup of coffee, accepted the plate of scrambled eggs he fetched from the sideboard and wished him good morning in a polite voice.

'Feeling better?' he enquired in a breezy manner which annoyed her at once. 'There's nothing like a good night's sleep to help one regain a normal view of things.'

She buttered toast and ate a mouthful of egg. 'My view of things is exactly the same as it was yesterday evening,' she told him frostily. 'I see no point in discussing it any more.'

'Not at the moment, perhaps. You still persist in your absurd accusations, Arabella?' His voice was smooth but it had a nasty edge to it. She reflected with a tiny shiver that he must have a nasty temper beneath that calm visage. Not that he could frighten her, she told herself silently.

She said clearly, 'Yes—and they are not absurd. You told me yourself in Holland that Geraldine was one of the most honest and dependable doctors you had ever met. You're not going to accuse her of lying, are you?'

He glanced at his watch and didn't answer her. 'I must go, I've a good deal to get through today. I'll be home by six o'clock, barring accidents. We are to dine with the Marshalls, aren't we?'

'Yes.'

'Good. In a day or two, when you've calmed down, we can have a quiet talk.'

'I do not want a quiet talk,' said Arabella pettishly. 'I can think of nothing more to say.'

'That astonishes me. I, on the other hand, have a great deal to say. Time enough to say it when we are at the manor.'

He put a hand on her shoulder as he went to the door and the touch of it sent sudden tears to her eyes. She loved him so, and she was behaving in all the wrong ways. She wasn't sure quite *how* to behave; he hadn't been very nice about her being sweet and forgiving...

Christmas was very near now; she wrapped some more presents, arranged Christmas cards all over the drawing-room—for they had been sent any number— and spent a long time making a centrepiece for the table with holly and Christmas roses and trails of ivy and sweet-scented hyacinths. It looked pretty when she had finished it and so did the small Christmas tree standing in front of the window, with its twinkling lights and glass baubles.

Tomorrow, she remembered, several of the doctors' wives were coming for coffee; she had met them at the Marshalls' and at the party and they had offered to tell her about the various festivities which would take place at the hospital after Christmas—to have them in for coffee had seemed a good idea. She was aware that they were curious about her but too polite to show it, and it would be nice if she could become one of their circle.

She took the dogs for a walk then, and presently set out for the last of her shopping. A present for Titus. She had left it until last, hoping to gain some

inspiration as to what he would like. He seemed to
have everything; the only thing was to go and look in
shop windows and hope to see something.

She might be angry with him and unhappy too, but
she loved him despite that. It would have to be something very special. She went from one end of Bond
Street to the other and down the arcades, peering in
windows—what did one give a man who had
everything?

She found it at last in a small bookshop, crammed
to the ceiling with rare editions, old maps and prints.
An early edition of Chaucer's *Canterbury Tales* in its
original text; she remembered that he had mentioned
his interest in the book and as far as she knew he had
only a modern version of it. She bore it home, reflecting sadly that perhaps this would be the last and
only present she would give him. She had an un-
pleasant feeling that the quiet talk he had suggested
might disclose a future she had no wish to
contemplate.

In the meanwhile there was the Marshalls' dinner-
party that evening. She dressed with extra care—dark
green velvet this time, long-sleeved and high-necked,
and since she had the time she arranged her hair in a
complicated topknot which was well worth the time
it took to do.

Titus was home when she went downstairs to the
drawing-room. He was sitting with the dogs, reading
the afternoon's post, but he got up when she went in.

'I'll go and change. Have the dogs been out?'

She put Percy down by the fire. 'Yes, they've had
their walk.'

'Good. Can I get you a drink?'

'No, thank you.'

She sat down and Percy got on to her lap and Bassett danced around her chair.

'You have enjoyed your day?' he asked.

'Yes, thank you. Several people are coming in for coffee tomorrow morning...'

'I shall be away all day, probably until late in the evening. Don't wait up for me tomorrow.'

'I expect you're busy,' she said politely.

'Yes, I have to go over to Leiden in the morning but I shall be back in good time to drive to the manor.'

He went out of the room, leaving her suddenly ice-cold with panic. He was going to see Geraldine, of course, and tell her what had happened, and when he came back they would have their talk and her heart would be broken.

The dinner party at the Marshalls' house was fairly small and she had met everyone there already. The house was decorated with holly and mistletoe and paper chains and an enormous Christmas tree and the atmosphere was decidedly festive. Dinner was leisurely and the talk was light-hearted and afterwards everyone gathered in the drawing-room, still talking. It was late when finally everyone went home, calling the season's greetings to each other as they went.

Back in the house Arabella said, 'That was a lovely evening; I enjoyed it.' She stood in the hall, looking at him. 'I'll go to bed. Will you be leaving early in the morning?'

'Yes. Shall I give your love to Cressida?'

'Oh, will you be seeing her?'

'Yes. Who did you suppose I'd be seeing, Arabella?'

'Well, Geraldine, of course.'

'Ah, yes, of course.' He turned away to go to his study. 'Goodnight, Arabella.'

There he sat, doing nothing behind his great desk. A brilliantly clever man, he hadn't been clever enough to know when he had fallen in love with Arabella. He supposed, since she had never been out of his mind for long since the moment they had first met, that he had loved her at first sight, unaware of it even when he had asked her to be his wife, knowing only that it was something which he wanted.

He gently pulled Bassett's small ears, for the little dog had climbed on to his knee, and then reached down to rest a hand on Beauty's head.

'When I get back,' he told them, 'we must talk, Arabella and I. Perhaps once we have cleared up this misunderstanding she could learn to love me.'

Arabella went down to her solitary breakfast, determined to fill her day so that there would be no time to sit and brood. There were the last of the presents to wrap and plans to make with Mrs Turner, who would stay in the house over Christmas. Not alone, however. Her married sister and her husband would stay with her and Arabella, prompted by Titus, had seen to it that there was an abundance of Christmas fare for them. Titus had several appointments for the day after Boxing Day and they had planned to return to Little Venice very late on Boxing Day. She wondered now, as she listened with half an ear to Mrs Turner's plans for a meal for them on their return, if it would be a good idea if she were to stay at the manor for a while. It would seem a natural thing to do and, in the light of the present situation, sensible too.

The day seemed long despite her efforts to keep busy. She had just got back from walking the dogs when the phone rang. Titus's cool voice sounded very close. He would be unable to get back home that evening—he hoped to be back some time the following afternoon. He would go straight to the hospital where he had a clinic and see her later. 'You are all right?' he wanted to know.

'Yes, thank you,' said Arabella. Even if she could have thought of something to say he didn't give her the chance. His goodbye was brief.

She spent the evening deciding what to take with her to the manor, although her mood was such that packing a couple of sacks would have done very nicely. The day was neverending; the coffee morning had taken up part of it, of course and she had laughed and talked and rather liked her guests and squirmed inwardly at their smiling remarks about brides and a rosy future. Medical men made rather good fathers, one of them had observed, amid laughter. She remembered that now.

Titus got home early the next afternoon, coming in unexpectedly on his way to the hospital. Arabella, tying an artistic bow on the parcel in which she had wrapped Mrs Turner's Christmas present—a handsome dressing-gown—looked up in surprise as he came in.

'I need something from the study,' he explained. 'I'll be home just after five o'clock. Will you be ready to leave shortly after that?'

'Yes. Would you like something before we go? Sandwiches and coffee? Tea?'

'I'll get tea at the hospital—we can have a meal when we get home. Phone Butter, will you? Tell him we'll be there about eight o'clock and will need supper.'

He had spoken pleasantly but she could see that he was impatient to be gone. Her, 'Very well,' was uttered in a matter-of-fact voice although her hands were shaking under the bunch of ribbons.

They left well before six o'clock after giving Mrs Turner her present, loading the boot with things for the manor and stowing the dogs and Percy on the back seat. The streets were crowded with Christmas traffic and it took some time to reach the motorway, and all the while Titus had nothing to say.

Arabella had tried once or twice to start up a conversation but since she received only pleasant monosyllables in reply she had lapsed into silence. Christmas, she thought bitterly. Last Christmas had been a terrible one, with her parents recently dead and the future bleak, but this one was even worse; the future was just as bleak. How could it be otherwise, loving a man who loved someone else?

CHAPTER NINE

THERE was a Christmas tree ablaze with lights just inside the gates of the manor when they reached it, and lights streamed from the many windows of the house. As they stopped before the door Arabella could hear Duke's deep bark and then was almost deafened by the happy barks of Beauty and Bassett. Titus got out, opened her door and let the animals out of the back of the car, picking up Percy's basket at the same time. Just for a moment Arabella stood looking around her; the door had been opened and Duke had come pelting out to greet them and then tear round the garden with the other two. Butter stood at the door and beyond him she could glimpse another Christmas tree in the hall. She heaved a sigh and Titus gave her a quick look which she didn't see.

Butter stood with a beaming face. 'Welcome home, ma'am—and you, sir. There's a nice little supper waiting for you when you're ready and Mrs Tavener Senior hopes that she and Miss Welling may share it with you.'

'Why, of course,' cried Arabella. 'Nothing would be nicer. I'll just take off my things and say hello to Mrs Butter.'

Titus had been taking Percy out of his basket; she took the cat in her arms and went off to the kitchen, glad to get away from Titus's blue stare.

They all had supper together shortly after and even Miss Welling looked cheerful and drank two glasses of wine. Old Mrs Tavener was full of questions which the doctor answered readily enough, referring often to Arabella to bear him out; whatever their differences were in private, they were to be kept that way.

The old lady went to bed presently with the faithful Miss Welling, very slightly tipsy, in attendance.

'I should like to talk,' observed Titus, 'but I think you have no wish to listen for the moment.'

'Well, no.' She sat down near the fire in the drawing-room with Percy curled up on her lap. 'I think I am still angry and hurt—if you wouldn't mind waiting a few days, until I feel all right again, I'll listen . . .'

'But you will agree with me that the hatchet should be buried over Christmas. I would not like Grandmother to be made unhappy nor would I like the painstaking preparations taken by the staff to be overshadowed; they have been here for so long that they are quick to sense when anything has gone wrong.'

She said quietly, 'Of course I agree with you. I'll do everything to make it as you wish.' She paused. 'Titus, may I stay here for a few days after Christmas? Just until you come on the following weekend. I think it might be a good idea, don't you?'

When he didn't reply she added, 'It's easier—I mean looking at something from a distance. Do you see?'

'Oh, yes, but surely that depends on how you are looking at it? Clearly and honestly or blinded by all the wrong feelings?'

'Feelings? Feelings?' Arabella wanted to know in a lamentably shrill voice. 'And you're the one who's blind.' She got to her feet, dislodging Percy who stalked to the door. 'I'm rather tired. Good-night, Titus.'

He was at the door before she could reach it. He was smiling a little and had kissed her before she could turn her head. 'Crosspatch,' he said, and actually laughed.

Which, naturally enough, caused her to burst into tears the moment she got into her room.

Feelings or no feelings, she woke on Christmas Eve knowing that they must be hidden. Besides the extra bustle in the house the carol singers would be coming in the early evening, she would be going to the church with an armful of flowers specially grown in the glass-house and there was a Christmas lunch for the children in the village hall at noon. A busy day and she thanked heaven for it.

She dressed carefully, knowing that it was expected of her, and Titus nodded approval when they met at breakfast. 'I'll see you at the children's party,' he told her pleasantly, for all the world as though they had parted the best of friends. 'I've one or two things to attend to first while you're in church.' He added, 'We go to the midnight service, Arabella. Grandmother and Miss Welling come too, and so do the Butters.'

She thought she detected a warning note in his quiet voice. 'I shall enjoy that. Do we go to the morning service as well?'

'Yes. It makes a full morning so we usually exchange our gifts when we get back here around noon, before lunch. I dare say you've already seen Mrs Butter?'

'Yes, she's arranged everything beautifully.'

'She was the kitchenmaid here when Grandmother came here as a bride. She must have been very young—thirteen or fourteen, I suppose. She has been here every Christmas since then.'

'But she married Butter...'

'There was a butler in those days—servants were two a penny—Butter worked under him until he learned to drive and he's been driving ever since and running the place for me. He's more than a servant, he's an old friend—so is Mrs Butter. She used to give me slices of bread and dripping—I was always hungry, and dripping in those days was delicious...'

Arabella looked down at her plate, picturing a small hungry boy wolfing bread and dripping. 'You were happy here?' she asked.

'Yes. And I shall be again.' He added silkily, 'I cannot say that at the moment I am happy.'

'Well, nor am I,' said Arabella in what she hoped was a reasonable voice. Perhaps this was the right moment to talk—over a prosaic breakfast table in the cold light of the morning.

It seemed that it wasn't; Butter came in to say that the flowers had been brought up from the glasshouse and perhaps she would care to approve them when she had breakfasted.

'I'll come now. I've finished,' said Arabella, all of a sudden anxious to escape from Titus, sitting so close to her and yet so far away.

The flowers were beautiful and she was lavish in her praise. 'I'll take them with me now. I'm going to church early—they'll need to be arranged.'

She put on the new winter coat and added the hat she had bought in a fit of extravagance. It was of the softest felt with a narrow brim which curved around her face and tilted very slightly sideways. It matched the coat exactly and she was well pleased with it. She was pleased with her boots too—of the very latest style, making the most of her small feet—and since it was Christmas she tucked a green scarf patterned with holly into the neck of the coat. Surveying her person in the pier glass, she thought that she didn't look too bad—not that Titus would notice, she reflected, and went downstairs.

He was in the hall, huge in his overcoat, waiting for her.

'Shall we walk down?' he asked her.

Since Butter was hovering, ready to open the door, she said at once, 'Oh, yes, I should like that. Will you take the dogs?'

'Of course. We'll part company at the church—I dare say you'll be some time there. We're expected for coffee at the rectory at eleven o'clock; we'll meet there.'

They went out together and Butter watched them go and thought what a splendid couple they made. Trust the doctor to get himself such a perfect little lady...

Arabella, walking beside Titus out of the gates and into the lane leading to the village, was surprised to find that despite their quarrel she felt quite at ease with him, listening to his easy flow of casual talk. And he, used to putting patients at their ease, watched her expressive face and was satisfied.

He left her at the church after a brief talk—his arm around her shoulder—with the rector, and she was led away to see about the flowers while the rector enlarged upon the doctor's splendid character. 'Takes after his father,' he told her. 'Does a great deal for the village, you know, and very much dislikes anyone finding out about it.' He beamed at Arabella. 'But of course he has no secrets from you, my dear Mrs Tavener.'

She and Titus met again at the rectory where they had coffee, surrounded by the rector's son and daughter-in-law and their children, all talking at once and plying them with mince pies.

Arabella, led away to tidy herself before going to the village hall, remembered that Titus's various aunts and uncles would arrive at teatime and wondered if they'd be as much fun as the rector's household. She adjusted the hat, powdered her nose and accompanied Titus through the village once more.

The children's lunch was noisy; the little boys tended to fight among themselves and the little girls, in their best dresses, were shy to start with and then noisier than the boys. They ate everything on the long table and drank enormous quantities of lemonade before pulling the crackers, putting on paper hats and crowding round the Christmas tree to receive the parcels Arabella was to hand to each of them.

She was enjoying herself mightily; she had taken off her coat, put a paper hat on top of her own elegant headgear and was singing along with the children in a small clear voice.

Titus was enchanted. The world was a wonderful place in which to be and only he and Arabella were in it. He smiled a little—he was a little too old to have such romantic thoughts. If only she would let him explain about Geraldine—but he would have to wait for the right moment to do that. In the meantime they must hide their differences for a couple of days, and perhaps her idea of staying at the manor for a few days was a good one...

They went back home presently, with the dogs running free around them, and had sherry with Mrs Tavener and Miss Welling. They ate their lunch with a good appetite and much cheerful small-talk then separated to go their own ways—Mrs Tavener to rest, with Miss Welling to read aloud to her, Titus to his study and Arabella to tour the guest-rooms to make sure that everything was just as it should be. There would be six guests staying over Christmas and eight more coming to lunch on Boxing Day.

She went to look out of the window of the largest room overlooking the grounds at the back of the house and saw Titus strolling around with the dogs. He looked very much at home in elderly, beautifully tailored tweeds, his hands in his pockets. He was whistling too. The wish to join him was very great. If she did, she reflected, he would greet her with apparent pleasure and set himself out to entertain her with a gentle flow of talk. He would probably wish her at Jericho. She went down to the kitchen and spent the next half-hour conferring with Mrs Butter.

The guests arrived for tea—first Mrs Tavener's son, a very upright grey-haired man with a reserved manner, who shook Arabella's hand and begged her to call him Uncle Tom, and his wife, Aunt Mary, who peered at her through thick lenses and murmured softly that it was a great pity that Jeremy Titus and Rosa weren't there to see their daughter-in-law.

'My father and mother,' said Titus briskly. 'Uncle Tom is the younger son. Come and meet the cousins.' They were three young men and a girl of her own age. 'Josephine, Bill, Thomas and Mark.' She shook hands with them in turn, aware of their interested gaze.

It was Thomas who spoke, a serious-looking young man who looked as though smiling was an effort. 'We were beginning to think that Titus would never marry...'

'Head of the family and all that,' explained Mark. 'Wish I'd seen you first.' He was a cheerful young man with an engaging grin. 'I'm a medical man too—haven't had time to get married, let alone find a girl to love as yet.' He nodded towards Thomas. 'He's just got engaged and Josephine is on the brink. Before we know where we are the family gatherings will be littered with babies.'

Everyone laughed, even Thomas, and after that the talk became general over tea round the fire. Presently Arabella went away to help Mrs Butter with the dinner table; they had discussed the menu over the phone some time ago and had decided on smoked salmon, rack of lamb with several vegetables and sauté potatoes, and a trifle for dessert. The table looked charming with a starched linen cloth, the family silver, a centrepiece of holly, ringed around by red candles in silver candlesticks, and sparkling crystal glasses. She went away to change her dress, feeling well pleased.

It was after one o'clock by the time she was in bed. The church had been full and no one had hurried away afterwards but had stayed, exchanging good wishes, and old Mrs Tavener had had to be coaxed away and driven back. Arabella had accompanied her and Miss Welling to her own rooms and seen her safely settled with a warm drink.

'You're a dear child,' the old lady had declared. 'Titus is a lucky man.'

He might not agree with that, reflected Arabella in the morning, accepting a cup of hot chocolate from him and sitting down beside Aunt Mary, but he was behaving exactly as he should—the smiling glance, the hand on her shoulder—almost as if he meant it.

Breakfast was leisurely before church and it was only when they got back that the family, with the Butters, gathered round the Christmas tree. Arabella and Titus handed out the presents together and since everyone had brought a gift for everyone else the drawing-room was soon knee-deep in coloured paper. It wasn't until the last of the presents had been handed out that Arabella sat down to open her own pile.

'Move over,' said Titus and sat down beside her on one of the sofas while Butter went round with a tray of champagne. 'I wonder why one has such pleasure in opening parcels?'

'Natural curiosity.' Arabella was admiring a rose-pink silk scarf from Josephine. 'Exactly what I would like best,' she told her new cousin. They were going to get on well together, she and Josephine. They smiled at each other across the room and she picked up the next gift. She had seen quickly enough the little box with its label written in Titus's hand and deliberately left it until the last. There had been presents from the dogs and from Percy of course—chocolates, perfume, a little evening bag—and of course he had bought those, just as she had given him a Victorian ink-blotter for his desk from the four of them. Everyone else was still opening gifts and no one was watching them. She felt his hand on hers for a moment. 'How did you know,' he asked her quietly, 'that I collect rare books?'

'I looked round the library here and at Little Venice. I hope you'll like it.'

'I am delighted with it, Arabella. Thank you, my dear.'

She opened the little box then. There were earrings inside, diamonds set in gold, miniature replicas of the necklace.

She held them up. 'They're beautiful, and they match the necklace——' She looked a question.

'I had them made ...'

'But you gave me the necklace only a week or two ago.'

He said patiently, 'I knew I would give you the necklace—oh, before we married—and it seemed that the earrings would go very well with it.'

'You did that before——' she paused and went on softly '— before you—before we went to Holland?'

She choked back tears and Mark called across the room, 'You two—what are you whispering about? Arabella, what has Titus given you? It must be something marvellous to make you look so bright-eyed.'

She got up and went to sit by him, taking the earrings with her, and everyone crowded round to see them. 'You must wear them,' cried Aunt Mary. So Arabella went to the Florentine mirror between the windows and put them on and someone cried, 'Aren't you going to thank him for them? Go on, it's Christmas.'

There was nothing for it but to go over to the sofa. Titus had got to his feet and she stretched up to kiss his cheek. At least, that had been her intention. Instead she found herself swept into his arms and kissed in a manner which took her breath away.

'Oh,' squeaked Arabella, and stared up into his face. His eyes were very blue and the gleam in them was no longer hidden.

'A pity we aren't alone,' he said softly, and let her go amid an outburst of cheerful teasing and laughter.

The rest of the day didn't seem quite real to Arabella. Lunch had been a buffet with everyone milling around—talking about their presents, recalling other Christmases, discussing the rest of the family who would arrive in time for tea. Tea had gone off well too, with a host of new faces and names to remember and the cake to cut, and then a brief peace while those staying in the house went upstairs to change for dinner. She had worn the brown dress with the diamond necklace and the earrings and there had been a lot more talk while they had drunk champagne cocktails and then gathered round the table to eat turkey with all the trimmings and one of Mrs Butter's Christmas puddings. She had sat opposite Titus at the oval table and tried not to look at him, something which she found very difficult.

Boxing Day, with a house overflowing with guests and several people from the village coming in for drinks, kept her so busy that she had no time to talk to Titus—which was a good thing. She was still feeling shy about his kiss and puzzled too, although perhaps he had kissed her like that because the family was watching. When they were alone again she would ask him—they still had to talk about Geraldine...

He went back to Little Venice after dinner on Boxing Day, leaving her there until he came to fetch her at the weekend. She went with him to the door after he had said goodbye to his family in the drawing-room.

'Well, we buried the hatchet very well, didn't we?' he observed, standing close to her, looking down on to the top of her head, smiling a little.

'Well, I think...' began Arabella, to be stilled by the ringing of the phone on the side table.

Titus picked it up. 'Mrs Turner? Is something wrong?' He listened a moment. 'From Leiden? You said I would be back later tonight—good.' He glanced at his watch. 'I should be with you in two or three hours.'

He hung up and Arabella said, 'That was Geraldine . . .'

He gave her a cold stare, his face expressionless. 'If you say so, Arabella . . .'

He went out to his car without a word, not looking at her, and because she loved him so much she knew instinctively that he was in a white-hot rage. 'Take care, Titus, oh, do take care . . . !'

He drove away without a glance and she stood shivering on the step until the tail-lights had disappeared. It was a good thing that when she returned to her guests her white face was attributed to her having to part with Titus. She was surrounded by people intent on cheering her up, plying her with drink and the suggestion that she should go to bed and have a good night's rest.

'All the excitement,' said Aunt Mary. 'You must be worn out. And you've made such a success of it, my dear. We all understand how you feel, it's hard to be parted, but doctors' wives . . .'

Everyone went home after lunch the following day and Mrs Tavener and Miss Welling retired to their own part of the house, which left Arabella with the three dogs and Percy for company. She had phoned Little Venice early that morning and Mrs Turner had told her that the doctor had left for the hospital not half an hour since. 'Looked worn out, he did,' Mrs Turner had said. 'A good thing when it's the weekend and he can fetch you back. And all that telephoning just when he should have been going to his bed . . .'

'Oh, yes,' Arabella had said, 'the call from Leiden . . .'

'That's right, madam. Went on and on, it did. Must have been about a patient, I suppose, because I heard him say he'd ring later.'

It was a phone call Arabella wished she hadn't made, for it only made the day harder to get through. A long walk with the dogs made her feel better. She had tea by the fire in the little sitting-room with Percy on her lap and the dogs hugging the fire and, since the Butters were going to the village for an evening with friends there, she had undertaken to see to her own dinner.

She busied herself presently in the kitchen—making a salad, cooking scrambled eggs and making a pot of coffee. She ate at the kitchen table, tidied everything away and went back to watch TV, but after a while she switched off and, suddenly making up her mind, phoned Little Venice. Mrs Turner answered again.

She sounded puzzled when Arabella asked to speak to the doctor. 'He's gone to Holland, madam—in a terrible rush, he was. Expects to be back tomorrow some time. I expect he'll phone you from there.'

Her voice held a faint question, so that Arabella said at once, 'I'm sure that he will—if he had a plane to catch he wouldn't have had the time to do a lot of explaining. I shall hear all about it when he gets back and I'm sure he'll phone here once he has the chance. It might be something urgent.'

It was a good thing she was on her own, she reflected, for there was time to think. How he must have disliked having to spend Christmas here, being the perfect host and the perfect husband, she thought. I dare say he made the excuse of work at the hospital so that he could get back as soon as possible. I wonder

what she said that made him to go Leiden in such a
hurry?

Arabella picked up the magazine lying on the table
beside her and began to tear it into ribbons. The ex-
ercise gave her a certain amount of satisfaction
although she would have much preferred the magazine
to have been Geraldine. It relieved her feelings a little,
although a few good screams would have been a great
relief.

There were two days to get through before Titus
would come. She filled them with almost unceasing
activity—grooming the pony and the donkey, going
for long walks with the dogs, visiting the rectory to
say what a delightful Christmas it had been, enter-
taining various ladies from the village anxious to enrol
her in the WI, the first-aid classes, the committee for
the annual church bazaar...

Friday came at last and no news from Titus. All
the same she had a long session with Mrs Butter about
meals for the weekend, saying lightly that she thought
he would probably be home late that evening and arranging a light supper for him. She was filled with
excitement at the thought of seeing him again even
though a quarrel seemed inevitable and her heart,
already badly cracked, would be broken completely.
A good thing to get it over, she told herself, and took
the dogs for yet another walk.

It was late afternoon when she suddenly decided
that she couldn't face him. She would go out and walk
up the lane behind the house from where she would
be able to see the lights of the car. Only when he was
in the house would she return. The Butters were in
the dining-room so she went to the kitchen and
through its doors to a passage lined with small

rooms—the pantry, the old-fashioned still-room, the larder, the boot-room. At the end of the passage was another door, leading to the kitchen gardens, behind which were a variety of elderly coats, old hats and, ranged beneath them, a selection of wellies. She got into a jacket with a hood, pushed her feet into Mrs Butter's wellies and went outside.

It was still light although there was a bank of cloud beyond the hills. For a moment she wondered if she should fetch a torch, but supposing Titus was to arrive early and meet her? She buttoned the jacket tightly and set off.

The lane up the hill beyond the kitchen garden was a stiff climb, and she marched to it via the stables so that she might offer carrots pulled from the garden to Bess and Jerry. By the time she was almost at the top, with the thick crown of trees which topped the hill only a few yards away, it was dusk, the distant clouds suddenly overhead and the first few drops of rain falling. As she stood looking down the hill towards the village there was a sudden gust of wind and the trees behind her swayed and creaked as it soughed through them. Though not a nervous girl, she wanted to be home—secure by the fireside.

There was a shortcut down the hill, a narrow path which she and Titus had once taken; it would mean going a little way up into the trees but she thought that she could find it even in the gathering gloom. Somewhere on the right of her, she decided, as the first of the trees closed over her. The rain was coming down in earnest now and turning to sleet as the wind freshened. She took the path and at the fork a few yards further turned to the left, towards the village,

took a step forward and rolled into a deep gully—
right to the bottom.

It was filled with dead leaves and an inch or so of
water. She lay where she was for a moment, too surprised to do anything, and then got slowly to her feet,
brushed herself down and looked for a way to climb
out. It wasn't a very deep gully but its sides were
slippery with wet bracken and earth and when she took
hold of a tuft of coarse grass it came away in her
hand and landed her in a puddle of water. She would
have to climb out before it got really dark so she went
carefully all round it, feeling for a foothold in its sides,
and came to the conclusion that there weren't any—
nor were there any large stones which she could pile
against its steep sides.

'How very unfortunate,' said Arabella. Not a
panicky person by nature, she felt a nasty little pang
of fear at the idea of spending the night there. Not
that she would have to do that, she told herself ro-
bustly. They would miss her at the manor. A pity she
hadn't brought a torch. If the wind would die down
she could shout, but at the moment it would be a
waste of breath. It just needs a rat or two, she thought
gloomily.

The doctor stopped before his home with a sigh of
satisfaction. Whether she liked it or not, Arabella and
he were going to have that talk—but first of all he
would wring her darling little neck and kiss her
silent . . .

He was welcomed by the three dogs with delight
and by Percy with dignity and then by the Butters in
their turn, beaming at him, deploring the sudden on-
slaught of bad weather and at the same time offering

tea, drinks and saying madam was in the drawing-room.

Only she wasn't. 'Well,' said Mrs Butter, 'she had a cup of tea here earlier, after she took the dogs out. She'll be upstairs. I'll call her.'

'Don't bother, I'll go,' said Titus and went up the staircase two at a time, knocked on the door and went in. Arabella wasn't there, of course; he went from room to room and then downstairs again. She wasn't there either.

'She wouldn't go out,' declared Mrs Butter. 'She took the dogs like I said, and I'd have heard the front door for we were both in the dining-room and you can hear it close from there.'

The doctor said, 'Ah, the back door,' and went to look, the Butters close behind. 'Is there anything missing?' he wanted to know, turning over the coats and capes hanging there.

'My boots,' said Mrs Butter suddenly. 'I had them on this morning—they were here, under that old jacket—I wear when I go down to the kitchen garden.'

'Take a torch, Butter, and go down to the village. See if anyone has seen Mrs Tavener. I'll go up the lane. Wave the torch if you find her—I'll do the same.'

He shrugged into an old mac, gave up the idea of boots since none of them were large enough for his feet, took the torch Mrs Butter had fetched, and opened the door. The wind took his breath as he stood there, the dogs crowding round, anxious to help. They all went up the lane at a great rate with frequent stops while Titus bellowed, 'Arabella,' in a voice to rival the wind.

Arabella heard it. She was numb with cold and her feet, despite the wellies, were blocks of ice although she hadn't stood still. Indeed she had been scrambling in a fruitless manner up the sides of the gully and slipping down to the bottom again. She was frightened now and her answering shout had been no more than a squeak, but she tried again and was cheered to hear his shout in answer. A long minute later she saw the torch shining above her and looked up to see four pairs of eyes looking down at her.

The dogs barked, delighted to have found her, and the doctor said, 'Oh, you silly girl,' in such a tender voice that she very nearly burst into tears. She gulped them back. 'Don't any of you fall in,' she said.

Titus was examining the gully by the light of the torch. He bade the dogs sit and then said, 'Now, listen carefully, Arabella. Go to the end—that's it, as far as you can go—it's a little lower. I'm going to lie flat and reach down to you. Lift your arms as high as you can and I'll lift you out.'

'You won't be able to—I'm too heavy.'

He laughed. 'One of your more ridiculous remarks,' he said cheerfully. He waved the torch in the air in the hope that Butter would see it and stretched his considerable bulk on to the soaking ground. It was raining very hard now but he hardly seemed to notice that. He put his great arms down into the gully and caught Arabella's cold hands in his.

She landed in an untidy heap beside him, covered in mud and bits of bracken and grass and very wet. He got up and lifted her to her feet and she said in a small polite voice, 'Thank you, Titus,' and burst into tears. He held her close while she sniffed and snuffled in a manner totally devoid of any glamour, then she blew her small nose, mopped her face and said, 'Sorry.'

'My dearest darling girl,' said Titus, in a voice which she had never heard before. He might have said a great deal more only Butter came puffing up to join them. As it was he contented himself with a kiss which took her breath before observing, 'Mrs Tavener had fallen in the gully, Butter—she's wet and cold. Would you go ahead and ask Mrs Butter to get a warm bath ready? We'll be right behind you.'

Butter hurried off and Titus picked Arabella up as though she had been a feather duster and carried her back down the lane with the dogs trotting beside him.

'I can walk,' said Arabella. He had called her his dearest darling girl. Had that been to keep her spirits up? And what about that kiss? Something to remember lingeringly.

Mrs Butter was at the door and so was Butter, with glasses and a bottle of brandy. 'Ah,' said the doctor, putting Arabella down but not letting her go. 'Just what we all need.'

'I don't like brandy,' said Arabella.

A remark of which the doctor, quite rightly, took no notice. She drank it down under his impassive gaze before he picked her up again, this time without the jacket, and carried her upstairs.

Half an hour later, warm and dry and very clean, her still-damp hair hanging down her back, Arabella went downstairs. 'You're not to dress, madam,' Mrs Butter had said. 'Doctor says a warm dressing-gown and you're to go to bed early.' First, however, she had to face him across the dinner table.

Titus was waiting for her in the drawing-room. He looked as though he had never been near a gully in his life—the epitome of a well-heeled gentleman with time on his hands. She went slowly into the room. It would be hard to ask him about Geraldine but it had to be done. 'Titus . . .' she began.

He was across the room and she was in his arms before she could say another word. 'And before you say anything, my darling heart, I love you. I think that I always have only it didn't occur to me sooner . . . And before you fling Geraldine in my teeth, I do not care a jot for her—never have. If you hadn't been such a busybody, flinging me at her head at all hours of the day, you would have seen that for yourself. And, yes, I went to Holland—because Aldrik's mother has had a stroke.' He looked down at her. 'Well, my darling?'

'Well,' began Arabella, 'I love you, you see and I think I must have a jealous nature.'

'There are ways of curing you of that,' said Titus.

Neither of them saw the faithful Butter come to announce dinner and slide away again.

Presently Titus said, 'I shall always remember this day, my love.'

'Me, too,' said Arabella and kissed him just once more.

She was remembering that just eighteen months later, sitting on the window-seat in the drawing-room, an open letter in one hand, a very small baby tucked under the other arm. 'He's coming home, my poppet—listen . . .'

She began to read the letter again, out loud this time so that their son could hear it too, even though it meant nothing to his very small ears . . .

Dearest love,
    By the time you read this letter I shall be on my

way home. I have missed you so—the week has seemed like a lifetime without you. I picture you and our son sitting in the drawing-room reading this—I wonder if I am right? I cannot wait to be with you again.

Why, I wonder, do VIP patients always choose to be ill in far-flung places? He is recovering; he will be flown home some time next week and I shall be able to treat him without having to leave you both.

I am not sure at what time we shall land but I shall be with you at the earliest possible moment.

Titus—who loves you.

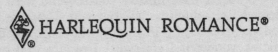

MILLION DOLLAR SWEEPSTAKES (III)

No purchase necessary. To enter the sweepstakes and receive the Free Books and Surprise Gift, follow the directions published and complete and mail your "Win A Fortune" Game Card. If not taking advantage of the book and gift offer or if the "Win A Fortune" Game Card is missing, you may enter by hand-printing your name and address on a 3" X 5" card and mailing it (limit: one entry per envelope) via First Class Mail to: Million Dollar Sweepstakes (III) "Win A Fortune" Game, P.O. Box 1867, Buffalo, NY 14269-1867, or Million Dollar Sweepstakes (III) "Win A Fortune" Game, P.O. Box 609, Fort Erie, Ontario L2A 5X3. When your entry is received, you will be assigned sweepstakes numbers. To be eligible entries must be received no later than March 31, 1996. No liability is assumed for printing errors or lost, late or misdirected entries. Odds of winning are determined by the number of eligible entries distributed and received.

Sweepstakes open to residents of the U.S. (except Puerto Rico), Canada, Europe and Taiwan who are 18 years of age or older. All applicable laws and regulations apply. Sweepstakes offer void wherever prohibited by law. Values of all prizes are in U.S. currency. This sweepstakes is presented by Torstar Corp, its subsidiaries and affiliates, in conjunction with book, merchandise and/or product offerings. For a copy of the official rules governing this sweepstakes offer, send a self-addressed, stamped envelope (WA residents need not affix return postage) to: MILLION DOLLAR SWEEPSTAKES (III) Rules, P.O. Box 4573, Blair, NE 68009, USA.

SWP-H495

HARLEQUIN ROMANCE®

brings you

Harlequin Romance #3361, *Mail-Order Bridegroom,*
in our Sealed with a Kiss series next month is by one of
our most popular authors, **Day Leclaire.**

Leah Hampton needs a husband for her ranch
to survive—a strictly no-nonsense business arrangement.
Advertising for one in the local newspaper makes good
sense, but she finds to her horror a reply from none other
than Hunter Pryde, the man she had been in love with
eight years before!

Is her fate sealed with one kiss? Or can she resist falling
in love with him all over again?

In the coming months, look for these exciting
Sealed with a Kiss stories:

Harlequin Romance #3366
P.S. I Love You by Valerie Parv in June

Harlequin Romance #3369
Wanted: Wife and Mother by Barbara McMahon in July

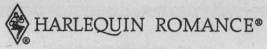